Twenty-Eight Vagabond Twenty-E

Series editor: Dana Keller

Three Kinds of Kissing

Helen Lamb

Vagabond Voices
Glasgow

First published in October 2018 by
Vagabond Voices Publishing Ltd.,
Glasgow,
Scotland.

ISBN 978-1-908251-91-6

Printed and bound in Poland

Cover design by Mark Mechan

Typeset by Park Productions

The publisher acknowledges subsidy towards this publication from
Creative Scotland and The Bridge Awards

For further information on Vagabond Voices, see the website,
www.vagabondvoices.co.uk

Lest we should see where we are,
Lost in a haunted wood,
Children afraid of the night
Who have never been happy or good.

W.H. Auden

Three Kinds of Kissing

1

1969

That May before Olive went to high school, she was five inches taller than me and ten months older, half an inch for every month. I still had to haul myself up and cling on by my fingertips to see the signal box behind the railway bridge. But Olive could see clear over the parapet and wave to the signalman.

If he looked up and shook his head, we wouldn't wait. He knew we weren't interested in the local trains that chugged to a halt at the station. It had to be an InterCity from Aberdeen or Inverness, whooshing straight through like the north wind. Long before we saw it, we heard the rumbling, held our breath while it grew into a roar. And as it blasted towards us, Olive yelled NOW and we let rip, bawling our lungs out, while carriage after carriage went shooting under us and the bridge shuddered.

I don't remember what I yelled. All I can remember now is Olive mouthing STOP. HELP.

*

1973

Four years on, the day after Olive goes missing, the railway bridge comes back to me, the burnt air rushing around us, blood buzzing. Her parents suspect she got on a train. They come to the door asking to speak to me and Mum says, "Of course." I don't get a choice.

They sit side by side on the settee and she takes the arm-chair opposite. I stay on my feet. Olive's dad says, "The two of you used to be close. Have you any idea where she might go?"

Mum says, "Think."

I shake my head. Olive stopped hanging around with me a long time ago.

Mum doesn't give up. "When did you speak to her last?"

"Tuesday morning, maybe, at the bus stop." But I'm not really sure. Olive and I got on the school bus at the same stop along with thirty or so other people. Sometimes we said hi, sometimes not. On the way back, she usually got off two stops before me in Station Road. One night last week though, she stayed on and we walked home together. It was the first time in ages. I don't mention this.

So far I haven't told a lie.

Her dad leans forward and stares at my mum. His eyes are bloodshot and fierce. "It was her birthday yesterday," he says. "Sixteen." He tells us it was also her day for the gym. She took her duffel bag as well as her school bag and set off for school as usual. That night, when her dinner lay cold on the table, they found her gym kit under her bed.

He squeezes his eyes shut tight now, and Olive's mum explodes. "What about the empty baked bean cans? What about the filthy spoon? It was a midden under that bed."

He flinches and frowns down at the floor. "Olive's mess, Olive's business, I thought we agreed."

Mum looks across at me. "We won't say a word now, will we Grace?"

He mumbles thanks, clears his throat and tells us how the police discovered Olive's school bag in the Ladies at the railway station, hidden in the waste bin beneath a heap of paper towels. Her uniform and black school shoes were stuffed inside. She had sixty-five pounds saved up from her Saturday job at the hairdresser's, as far as he knows, and only one change of clothes, including her green velvet jacket and cream patent shoes.

"No spare underpants," Olive's mum says. He goes to take her hand and she swats him away.

He says, "I don't think we can be sure of that." But she is adamant she can account for every pair. I believe she can too. That's the scary part.

This afternoon, I don't have any answers for Olive's parents. But they're only interested in *where* she went. They don't ask if I know *why*. After they leave, my mum says, "It's just like Gina Broadfoot to focus on the mess. You'd think she'd be more concerned about the secret eating." I'm scared she'll start quizzing me about Olive again but she lets me go out.

*

The river is the colour of Coca-Cola, fizzing and foaming round rocks in its way. On the western bank, the railway runs alongside. I race along the eastern bank till I come level with the island. It's not much to look at, a bunch of rocks and sand and scrub trees. Most of the year, the current's too fast to wade out there but days like today, when the river is low, a rough causeway of rubble appears. We used to jump over, boulder to boulder, Olive and me. We were always trying to get away from the ordinary world. I wanted adventures, and she would be looking for some new place to hide. Nowhere on the island was ever safe enough for her though. She said anyone who bothered to look could spot us from the bank.

I scan the island methodically now, foreground to background, left to right. Not that I expect to find her there but I still feel the need to check, rule it out, make sure she really has gone. Trust Olive to go on the run without sensible shoes. I picture her now on some strange city pavement, smiling down at her shiny shoes. They're cheering her up, cheering her on, reminding her she needs to keep going.

I turn away from the island and head into the scruffy patch of town between the river and the railway station, past the bookie's, the chippie, the post office, and through the beery reek around the Railway Arms. A train has just pulled in and I stop across the road from the station exit and watch all the shoppers and commuters straggling out. She could come back any time. That's the thing – any moment of any day, if not by train then by one of the buses that draw in at the stop outside the station. There's no guarantee she'll manage to stay away. She'd better try though. I won't be able to relax until I'm sure she's gone for good. I don't know what to think about the beans. Chocolate I would understand – but who eats beans in secret?

I decide to wait for the next train, and the next one, just in case. In between, I keep an eye on who gets off the buses. But there's no sign of Olive. More shoppers, more workers – that's all. Off home for dinner, they don't hang around and nobody notices how long I've been here. It's going on for six o'clock before I budge from my spot.

Halfway across the railway bridge, I pull a pack of Dad's cigarettes from my jacket pocket and strike a match, suck stolen smoke into my lungs. These days, I can see clear over the parapet and into the signal box where the signalman sits reading his newspaper behind the row of big wooden levers. I want him to notice me, look up and wave the way he used to when it was me and Olive. I want to feel the rush of energy only an express train can bring, but he's still reading when I finish the cigarette and throw the stub down on to the track. And I'm not ready to go home yet. I need more time to think.

The town gets newer as it climbs out of the valley. On the way up, I pass billboards advertising yet another new housing estate. They don't call them houses though. They are "executive villas", the three-bed Montrose, the four-bed Braemar. When the first incomers settled on the hill, Olive and I admired their big picture windows and the gardens all edged with identical concrete walls. We liked the sameness and we began to be ashamed of the mishmash of fences and stone dykes and hedges down our way. Soon we discovered the descending order of property: detached, semi-detached and terraced. The new houses were mostly detached and where we lived was terraced. Every year, we had to hike a bit further to get to the edge of town – the fields, the woods, the rutted lanes where we liked to roam.

Today when I get to the top of the hill, I stop and look back over the town. It's four years now since we were close but I still hang on to her secrets. The square we grew up in is easy to spot, right at the heart of a grid of terraced streets. Officially, Olive's only been gone for a day. No one but me understands how long she's really been lost.

2

1963

In the beginning, Olive needed a friend and she picked me. I was five and average height for my age. She was six but big as eight. She watched over the garden gate while I dangled a worm in front of my face and did my best to put her off. The worm shrunk upwards and shuddered in the breeze then slowly stretched as gravity pulled it down and down towards the black hole of my mouth. I swallowed it whole, eyes shut tight, and felt it slip and slide down my throat. When the wriggle finally reached my belly, my eyelids snapped open and I stared straight out at Olive Broadfoot.

Her red hair flickered in the sunlight. "What's it taste like?" she said.

I looked around the garden until I found a fat, juicy one with a bulging purple head. "Try one if you want to know." I held it out over the gate – and her hand shot up to her mouth.

"But it's alive."

I nodded and shoved it towards her.

She said, "I just want to watch."

So I had to show her again. I stuck out my tongue and let it slither in. Only, this time, she didn't seem so impressed. "*Now* can I come into your garden and play?" was all she had to say.

I shook my head. "I'm going inside." There was *Crackerjack!* on TV, and I didn't see why she was so interested in me anyway. She should get a friend her own age.

When Dad got home from work he agreed with me. Olive Broadfoot was too nosey and I was his favourite girl. Maybe Olive did have hair like red silk and mine was just ordinary brown, but he'd decided not to swap me for the girl across the square. He'd thought about it though, or he would not have said. I searched the creases in his smiling face. He had considered swapping me.

Mum said, "Don't look so worried. He's just kidding." She handed me a chocolate biscuit, but I knew I'd been compared and I had not come out the best. I bit into the biscuit and, deep down in my belly, I felt two little tickles. The worms were waiting to be fed.

Mum said to Dad, "Olive gets her hair washed every day. Gina told me she puts a drop of ammonia in the rinsing water to scare away the nits and give it that extra shine, the stuff I use to clean the lavatory. It's a wonder the child still has her eyesight." She ruffled my hair of straw and unwrapped a biscuit for herself. "Just this one," she said and popped it in her mouth.

Of course, we knew she didn't mean it. One biscuit was never enough, and Dad was always promising he would never swap her for a slimmer model. He must have thought about it though, or he would not have said.

The worms were squirming in my belly. They were hungry still. Mum would've screamed if she'd known. She caught me one time, licking a wee baby worm. She yelled over and over. *SPIT IT OUT. SPIT IT OUT. SPIT IT OUT.* And I got such a fright I bit right through its skin. The worms had to be secrets after that. Revolting things. I swallowed them to keep them safe. I took good care of them and all my other secrets too.

*

The worms would've been enough to put most folk off, but Olive couldn't take a hint. Once she got a thing about you, she wouldn't leave you be. On the way home from school next day, she caught up with me at the top of the high street.

"You're all alone," she said. "Did you fall out with your friends?"

I shook my head. I'd only been at school a week and I

didn't know anybody well enough to fall out with them yet.

She said, "Are you sure?"

I was sure.

But her eyes were full of pity. She linked her arm through mine and said, "I'll be your friend and get you home from now on."

I must've said okay. I don't remember now. All I know is *from now on* lasted for the next six years and we walked home together every day till Olive started high school. I do remember asking about her little brother. He was in my class and his name was Peter. Why didn't she walk home with him?

Olive said, "Don't be daft. I see enough of him already." She told me she would've preferred a sister but Peter was better than nothing, and she wouldn't want to be an only child, like me. If there was nothing on the telly, they sometimes played card games like Snap and Happy Families. "I slap him if he cheats," she said. She looked at me and laughed, and I felt her breath hot on my cheek. I didn't want to be that close to her.

3

1973

Friday morning and two days now since Olive went missing – soft May light glows through my eyelids, molten gold. I keep them closed and drift between sleep and waking until I hear the back door bang, the signal Mum's home from another night shift at the hospital. Her voice rises through the kitchen ceiling and buzzes round my bedroom, on and on and on. Something's up, but I can't make out what. Finally, Dad gets two words in.

"Marion......... PLEASE."

Now she starts slamming doors. She does that when she's mad at him. She puts things away in cupboards. Sometimes, if she's really mad, she calls for me to help and we both bang and slam. She talks to me and not to him, makes it sound like I'm on her side.

I turn on my radio to David Bowie singing "Starman", turn it up full blast, but I can still hear them. I drag myself out of bed and over to the window, peer out at the square – four blocks of terraced houses facing in on a patch of grass with a circular rose bed in the middle. The roses aren't out yet and a ginger cat is prowling among the thorns. I don't think it belongs round here. Each house is the same as the next except for the front doors which are painted alternating primary colours: red, yellow, blue, red, yellow, blue... Olive's family live across the square in a house that is a mirror image of ours except their door is yellow and our door is red. The last two nights, her bedroom curtains haven't been drawn. I squeeze my eyes tight shut and try to picture her on some crowded city street, Glasgow maybe, or London. She's tall for a girl, tall as a man. Green velvet jacket and slick patent shoes. Red hair glinting. She glances back at me for a second before she turns and darts into the forest of strangers.

I'm still at the window when the police car pulls up outside the Broadfoots' house and two policemen climb out, a constable and a sergeant. The sergeant is stocky. The constable's a lithe, blond giant. They tramp up the Broadfoots' path to the yellow door and the sergeant presses the bell. While they wait for an answer, the constable looks about the square. I get the feeling he already knows I'm here but he takes his time, glancing left, straight ahead, and right before he looks up at me and his eyes narrow, as if he suspects I'm somehow involved in Olive's disappearance. We stare at each other until Bill Broadfoot opens the door.

By the time I get downstairs, Dad has gone to catch the train and it looks like he left in a hurry. There's a half-drunk cup of coffee lying on the counter and a cigarette stub still smoking in the saucer. Mum sits slumped at the kitchen table nursing a glass of sherry. She doesn't look up, doesn't say good morning. The air is heavy with her mood. I ask if she's okay, terrified she might say no. She might start to tell me what's going on with her and Dad.

But she just says, "I'm weary."

I eye the sherry glass and say, "I'll make you tea."

I fill the kettle and get a clean cup from the shelf. While the water comes to the boil, I shake some cornflakes into a bowl and splash milk over them, eat them on my feet and, for once, she doesn't ask if that's all I'm having or nag me to sit at the table. The kettle switches off and I put down my bowl. She takes it extra weak, no milk, no sugar, just a quick dip of the teabag to give the liquid a bit of colour. I plonk the cup down in front of her, lift her glass, and at last she looks up at me. Glares. I pretend not to notice, try to ignore the rotten-sweet smell of her sherry dregs.

She says, "What time did he get in last night?"

"I'm not sure."

"Did you see him?"

"No. I went to bed early. I heard him though." This isn't true. I go to the sink and rinse out the glass.

"He should've been home for you."

"Mum, I'm fifteen. I was fine." I edge towards the kitchen door and hover there. I'll miss the school bus if I don't get a move on, but she's looking tearful.

"You don't have to go," she says. "Take the day off if you like."

But I do have to go. I tell her I have a maths test first thing. This *is* true and, right now, trigonometry doesn't seem so bad. I'd rather try to get my head round sine and tangents than my mother in this mood. She gets to her feet and unbuttons her white nurse's tunic, pulls it up over her head and pads across to the washing machine, stuffs a bundle of tea towels in along with it. She's shorter than me these days. I still can't get used to that and stripped down to her slip I can see she's softer too. I'm not sure who I'm protecting right now, her or Dad. I didn't hear him come in last night. That's nothing new.

She says, "You'd better get going then." And I nip back and give her a quick peck on the cheek, try not to look too relieved.

*

Claire and I sit in the front seat of the upper deck and, three rows back, Morag Ross's school bag sits in the empty space where Olive used to be. Morag has a receding chin and pale, fawn eyes that never look straight at you. Olive was her only friend and now she has nobody. Our double-decker bus rumbles northwest towards the grey-green mountains of the Trossachs. There are buses up ahead of us and more behind, in all a fleet of seven double-deckers and a single. The school catchment area takes in two main towns and a dozen villages, but only our town is growing. These days we make up more than half the high school roll.

Claire and I have sat together on the bus since we started high school nearly three years ago. Folk say we look alike but really it's just our hair, both straight and dark. I am sallow and she is rosy. I'm on the thin side and she has proper curves. Most lunchtimes we go down town to Gonnella's Café. Folk probably think that means we're close, but this morning when she says "Did you know Olive ran away?" I just nod. I don't tell her I already talked to Olive's mum and dad, or about the empty bean cans under Olive's bed.

Claire says, "I heard the police were round at Morag's house last night, and Morag claimed she didn't know where Olive was. D'you believe that?"

I shrug and glance round at Morag and, for a second, catch her looking back before her eyes slide away from me. If I didn't know better, I'd think she was hiding something. But Morag Ross knows nothing. Nothing important anyway. *Not the really private stuff* – that's what Olive said last week when we walked home together.

Claire takes out her maths book and starts practising trigonometry equations. I suppose I should do the same. Instead I sit and gaze out the window, and the grey-green mountains loom closer and closer.

4

1969

It must have been a Saturday, or maybe the summer holidays, the last time me and Olive climbed the hill to Pisgah Wood, because we had the whole afternoon. The sun glared out of the bare, blue sky and the air was still and clammy. Our cotton dresses clung to our damp skin. Our feet were on fire, and the skin on Olive's nose was pink and shiny with raggedy white edges where it was starting to peel.

"Staring's rude," she said. But her nose was in the middle of her face. Where else was I supposed to look?

She said there were ways of looking. There was no point arguing with her when she was in this kind of mood. We'd wanted to go swimming down at the dam that day, but Olive wasn't allowed because of the effluent from the dye works. Effluent was germs, according to her mum, and she hated germs. Her mum was never done cleaning, and not just the house, but Olive and her brother Peter as well. Olive said she didn't know when to stop. Some nights, in the bath, she scrubbed their knees with a nail brush and scouring powder and she scrubbed so hard they were still red-raw in the morning.

That afternoon on the way up to Pisgah Wood, Olive said her mum would put them in the washing machine too, if she thought she could get away with it. The whole bit. Pre-wash, hot wash, rinse and spin. Of course, they would be dead by the time they got to spin. But they would be clean. Dead clean. Clean forever and ever. She laughed and birled round and round like she was in the dryer.

In Pisgah Wood, we made a den in the middle of a rhododendron thicket and carpeted the floor with ferns. I soon got bored sitting there but Olive didn't want to move. She said she was fine just peering through the leaves.

I asked what she was looking for and she said, "Danger. If you don't watch out, you won't see it coming." I wanted to know what kind of danger and she said, "Use your imagination."

But I couldn't imagine. I could only think. "You'd probably hear it first," I said. "The danger – you'd hear it before you saw it."

She tutted. "Not if you keep talking I won't."

I left her to guard the den and went hunting for wild raspberries in the hedges at the edge of the wood, swallowing them as fast as I could pick them till my belly started nipping and I remembered Olive. She was always hungry, even hungrier than me. I gathered up the hem of my frock to make a pouch and filled it with berries to take back to her.

She didn't say thanks, just checked inside each raspberry for bugs and sucked them down one at a time while the dark red juice bled into my lap. She said, "It looks like you've been in an accident." And once she'd done eating, she had this idea to pretend I was dying and she would try and save me. I lay down on the ferny floor and she gave me the kiss of life and her mouth tasted of raspberries, both sweet and sharp together.

*

On Sunday afternoons, we didn't get out to play. I went to my gran's for tea and the Broadfoots went to view the latest show homes. I'd see them trooping out of the square, Olive and Peter in their best clothes, Bill Broadfoot stiff in shirt and suit, and Gina with her hair backcombed into a burnished auburn helmet. She'd just had a baby. His name was Bobby and Olive got to push his pram.

On the way to school on Monday mornings, she would tell me all about the fitted kitchens, the porches and the patios and the French windows. The show homes had beds where nobody slept, chairs and couches where nobody sat,

16

and tables where nobody ate. She said this was her mum's idea of heaven. Spotless forever. Her dad pretended to be interested to keep her mum happy but he was always looking out the windows. The baby slept through it all and Peter would chew bubblegum, while Olive made up stories in her head about the family who would live there soon. She gave them names and jobs and hobbies, favourite songs and favourite colours. And she told me, when her parents weren't looking, Peter would pull the wad of gum out of his mouth and stick it to the underside of the nearest chair or table. He left some in every show home.

She seemed to think this was normal behaviour for a boy. I wasn't sure. Maybe it was. I didn't have a brother.

*

It must have been another Saturday that summer when we broke into the old NAAFI canteen. We'd poked around outside before, peeked in the windows, and Olive always said it made her mad to see all that private space going to waste. The NAAFI was shoebox shaped, with a flat roof and rows of metal-framed windows on all four sides, and its scarred grey door was bolted and padlocked, top, middle and bottom. When the War was going on, soldiers camped out in the fields around it, but that was long before we were born. These days, it sat on its own down the bumpy rutted track between the blacksmith's and the mushroom farm. We'd never seen the mushrooms. They grew inside big sheds in the dark.

That afternoon, the forge doors were open and sparks of molten metal lit the blacksmith's silhouette. He had on goggles and we couldn't tell which way he was looking or if he saw us sneaking past. The stink of fertiliser from the mushroom farm was so strong we could taste it rancid on our tongues as we sprinted down the track.

We went round all the windows until we spotted a loose catch. It was too high to reach and Olive gave me a punt up.

It had to be that way round. I was lighter. She was stronger. I slid a stick between the outer and inner frame and tried to shove the catch upwards. The stick got jammed and snapped and Olive said, "What did you do that for?" Like it was my fault.

Next, we found a thin wedge of stone and she gave me another punt. I wiggled the stone beneath the catch till she started groaning that I was getting heavy. I shoved the stone harder then – and the catch sprung free. I ducked and pulled the window wide, heaved myself up. I was nearly in. And that was when we heard the barking.

I twisted my head round. Two Alsatians were bounding through the field towards us and a boy was racing after them yelling *HEEL... HEEL... HEEL...* But the dogs kept coming. And Olive let go of my foot, left me stuck half in, half out the window, with these huge dogs panting hot breath up my skirt and licking my bare legs.

I didn't know the boy. But she said, "Hiya Tony," like he was her friend or something. He came right up and stopped behind me and I couldn't see him any more. Olive asked what the dogs were called and he said Cain and Abel, and he sounded like he was smiling. She said hiya to his dogs next, and I could tell she was smiling too. She seemed to have forgotten whose side she was supposed to be on. The metal window frame was digging in between my ribs, and the dogs' slavers were running down my legs, and she just left me hanging there. They could've gobbled me alive for all she cared.

The boy shouted *DOWN* but the dogs didn't want to obey. He had to haul them back. He said, "They must like the taste of you. They don't lick just anyone."

I twisted my head round again and told him to get lost, and he grinned back at me. This boy had hair the colour of caramel. Olive probably thought he was good-looking, but his head looked too big to me. He had a skinny wee body and a great big head and they didn't fit together. If his head was any bigger, he would've looked like a cartoon and Olive wouldn't have gone all soft and gooey the minute she saw him. She'd have gone yuck instead.

He asked if he could come in with us and play, and I jumped down fast. I knew Olive would say yes, but I got in first and I said, "No – a boy would spoil it."

He smiled at me for a second then shrugged and turned away, loping off the way he came, and the dogs darted after him.

Olive glared at me. "What did you go and say that for?" She called out to him, "Grace is scared of dogs. Sorry. It's not you."

I wasn't sorry though.

*

It was quiet inside. We could hear ourselves breathing in and breathing out. The floor was piled with soft deep dust, silvery in the shadows, golden in the light. The room had windows on three sides and a wall with two green doors. After Tony went away, Olive said I hurt his feelings and his dogs were only being friendly. I didn't need to be so rude. It was okay for her. They never stuck their slobbery tongues up her skirt. She told me Tony was the blacksmith's son. She was surprised I didn't know. It wasn't like he was an incomer. His grandpa was Italian though, and his real name was Antonio. Plus she said he was THE most popular boy in her class. Everyone liked Tony, not just the boys, the girls as well. Then she went off into a side room and I was on my own.

She'd left a trail of footprints in the dust from the window we came in, round the edge of the room. They stopped at a green door. Closed now. But she hadn't slammed it shut. She'd closed it with a careful click, and this felt more serious somehow, like she wanted me to know she meant it and she wouldn't forgive me in a hurry.

Now the boy knew we were here, I couldn't relax. I stood by the window, watching out for him, listening for his dogs, while specks of dust danced in the air around me. You could cut right through them with your arm, make a clear space, make a wish, but you had to make it quick before the dust danced back again.

I wished that the dogs had never led him here.

I wished Olive would forget him, open the door and talk to me again.

When I couldn't stand the silence any more, I tiptoed across the dusty floor and turned the handle on the green door. She was standing with her back to me, looking through a window where she'd wiped a clear patch in the dirty glass. The sun was shining in and her hair was all lit up and fiery and, the second she turned round, I saw that she had secrets from me now. Her blue eyes were flecked with colours that weren't there before – turquoise, indigo and violet. And she had this private smile.

I said, "D'you want to play yet?"

She just shrugged.

"D'you want to go someplace else then?"

She shook her head.

I leaned against the wall and sighed.

"You don't have to stay," she said. "I'm not making you."

She turned back to the window. There was nothing to see out there except boulders and weeds, and I got the feeling she was hoping the boy might come back without the dogs. And maybe she wanted to kiss him. Or she wanted him to kiss her. Either way – she wouldn't want me around. I left her there to think about him. My footprints made a trail from the green door back to the window we came in.

5

1973

As soon as the trig test is over, Olive is back on my mind. There are fifteen minutes still to go before the end of class and Miss Morgan uses the time to show us how to solve oblique triangles, but I can't concentrate. The chalk squeaks as she writes on the blackboard: $A + B + C = \pi$. The hum of a mower over on the playing fields drifts through the open window. I breathe in the smell of fresh-cut grass and wonder if Olive's parents spoke to Morag Ross yet and if her mum mentioned the bean cans again. And I wonder why Olive was so hungry, and why baked beans, all that gloopy cold tomato sauce straight from the can. Yuck. I don't want Olive in my head but she won't go away.

Miss Morgan points at me now. She wants an answer, and I squint at the board. I don't have a clue.

"Work it out then."

That would be a good idea, if only I had heard the question.

"Make an attempt."

I look at her blankly and she glares back.

The true answer, as opposed to the right one, is *I DON'T CARE*. The trouble with maths is there can only be one answer. Not like real life. Take, for instance, the square root of Miss Morgan. How d'you work that one out? Her eyes are a bit watery today and her lipstick looks wobbly, like she might've been crying when she put it on. This morning when she walked in, some girls at the back of the class started sniggering, and I was almost sorry for her. I wanted to tell her to go and wipe the lipstick off. She's watching me still, and her eyes are steely underneath, and she only ever smiles when she's about to be sarcastic. Like now.

She bares her teeth and says, "A for apathy + B for bugbear = C me after class."

The period bell rings out and the rest of the class shuffle to their feet, stuff their jotters in their bags, and file out of the room. Now it's just me and Miss Morgan. She settles down behind her desk, gazes at me and sighs.

"Your work's been slipping," she says. "And why the attitude all of a sudden? Is something troubling you?"

I shrug and look away. A load of things are troubling me. Dad's absence last night. Mum's sherry glass this morning. The policemen at the Broadfoots' door. And all the places Olive could be, all our old hiding places where only I would know to look. She'd better not be there. She'd better be far away.

Miss Morgan says, "You can always talk to me."

She must be kidding. I can't talk to anyone. I can't think of anything that's safe enough to say. And since when did she start to be so understanding anyway?

She sighs again and gives me extra homework. I've to hand it in tomorrow. She's forgotten that tomorrow's Saturday.

The rest of the day, I worry about one thing after another. I worry that I've failed the trig test. I worry that one night soon Dad won't come home at all and I'll wake up to find it's just me and Mum. The thought of being left alone with her ties my stomach into knots. I worry about the constable on the Broadfoots' doorstep this morning and the way his eyes narrowed. I suspect he got a kick out of making me feel guilty. I worry that he'll find Olive and push her into coming home. I worry if she does come back what might come out then. I'm praying that she stays away. I worry that she's hungry right now. I'm so busy worrying I don't hear the French teacher telling me to take the gum out of my mouth until she strides up to my desk. She says something about dumb insolence and waves the wastepaper bin in my face. I gaze back at her like she's gone crazy and, for a second, go on chewing. So I get extra French homework too.

And Claire hisses, "What's wrong with you?"

On the way home, I skip off the bus two stops early at Station Road and wave up to Claire. She would've come with me if I'd let her and now she's peering down at me from the top deck, watching me just like I used to watch Olive all the times she got off here. Sometimes, Olive would look up and catch me being nosey and she would smile this tiny smile, the kind you could never quite work out. I can't say for sure where she used to go next, but I have a good idea.

*

Branching off Station Road into the gloom, there's the alley where Olive's grandma lives. At the bottom end, the road bridge spans the river. At the top, the footbridge arcs across the railway line. In between is a jumble of cottages. Her grandma's place is halfway in, where the shadows are thickest, a narrow house with just two windows, a casement at street level and a dormer above, both shrouded in dusty net curtains. Today I peer as I go by but I can't tell if anybody's in, and I'm not sure why I bothered, why I'm even here. What did I hope to see? All I know is I had to come. Olive has been in my head all day pulling me here.

This alley used to be a forbidden place. The quickest way from where we lived to the high street and the primary school, but Olive's mum said not to go near. No matter what, we had to go the long way round by Station Road and past the post office. I wanted Olive to ask why, but she always said there was no point. Her mum didn't answer questions that didn't suit her. You did as you were told and that was that. Even now, I can't shake off the feeling I'm not supposed to be here and I have to remind myself her mum's rules don't apply to me. They never did. I can go where I like. All the same, I'm glad to get out of the alley and back into the light. I race across the railway bridge and the rest of the way home.

In the square, Gina Broadfoot's out scrubbing her steps. She's wearing a pair of pink rubber gloves. It's only two days since Olive went missing but her mum's war on dirt goes on just the same. The three steps up to her front door are still the best-scrubbed steps in the square, the best-scrubbed steps in the streets around us, maybe in the whole town. She's going hard at it, backside swaying in time with the strokes of the scrubbing brush.

As soon as I get in, I hear Mum's voice. I stick my head around the living room door and wave hello, and she looks up, phone in one hand, sherry glass in the other. She shrugs at me, as if to say she can't wave back, and her housecoat falls open. I catch a glimpse of faded blue nightdress and duck back into the hall. Before I start up the stairs, I hear her say, "I've had enough, Marie."

So it's Marie again. Mum's been on the phone to her every night this week, a sure sign something's up. Marie and Mum went through their nurse's training together. She's Mum's oldest friend, and godmother to me. Since the christening, Dad's not been back inside the church and I don't think I've ever heard him mention God. I suspect he doesn't believe but he's too tactful to say. Mum's keen on God. She goes to church most Sundays on her own and, once in a while, Marie keeps her company.

On the landing wall, there's a black-and-white photo of Marie with a bundle in her arms that's supposed to be me, but you can't actually see me. It could be any old baby, or a doll, or a log of wood rolled up in the christening shawl. Mum told me once that Marie used to love to dance. Her jiving was wild, but she lost her oomph when she married Geoff and gave up nursing. Mum said that's what happens when you rely too much on a man. A woman should always have some money of her own. This is the only relationship advice she has ever given me, and I didn't really get it at the time. It seemed like a lame excuse for working nights when she didn't have to, but lately I've begun to grasp the power of money and the need to get hold of some. Even a little bit can have the power to change everything. Sixty-five pounds was enough help Olive vanish, gave her the choice. I have no money and no choice yet.

In my bedroom, I drop my school bag on the floor and go to the window in time to see Gina Broadfoot pour a pail of clear rinsing water over her front doorstep. Rivulets of soapy scum stream down her garden path. She stands in the doorway watching and, for a moment, her body slackens as though all her usual pent-up restlessness is flowing away along with the water. She peels off the pink rubber gloves and closes the yellow front door. She'd have a fit if she could see the state of my room right now – clothes strewn all over the floor, last night's pyjamas, yesterday's school shirt, tights and knickers. I leave it all where it is, dig my maths book out of my school bag and go downstairs to the kitchen.

The smell of sherry hits me before I see it. Harveys Bristol Cream. Mum has left the bottle lying open on the counter. I screw the lid back on tight and settle down at the kitchen table to do the extra trig.

When she finally gets off the phone, Mum comes through complaining Marie has no opinions of her own these days. "Whatever drivel Geoff spouts, Marie spouts as well," she says. "I might as well try to squeeze some sense out of a wet sponge."

It's Friday and she's off-duty tonight. She opens the sherry bottle and refills her glass, leaves the lid off again. She doesn't often drink in front of me but today she seems to have forgotten I'm not supposed to see. Most of the time, she keeps the bottle in her bedroom and I never let on I know. The sherry's meant to be a secret and it's up to both of us to keep it that way. I can't do it on my own. Right now, I don't want to look at her. I wish she'd go and put some clothes on. Instead she wanders over to the kitchen table and sits down opposite me.

"Yesterday," she says, "you didn't seem too surprised about Olive."

I go on gazing at my maths book.

"Look at me when I'm talking."

I raise my head and she tries to outstare me. She still

thinks she can pull that old trick. It used to work. She only had to give me one of those hard looks and I felt guilty. Of something. I wasn't always sure what. But I'm wise to her tactics these days. I stare straight back at her now and she's the first to blink.

"There's something you're not telling me," she says.

I have to stop myself from grinning. There's a load of stuff I don't tell her. Where would she like me to start?

She gazes down into her sherry glass and pushes it around in little circles. "It's strange Olive only took one change of clothes. No underpants, Gina said. Bill didn't want her going into that." She looks up quickly. "How many pairs do you have? I suppose I should know."

I shrug. I don't see why she should. I don't need that kind of attention.

"Selfish girl," Mum sighs and lifts her glass. "Olive, I mean, going off like that after what happened to her brother." She takes a swig of sherry. "Four years might seem a long time at her age, but not for her mum and dad. You never get over losing a child." I have to change the subject fast before she starts raking over how Peter died.

"I think I failed that maths test."

For a moment, she looks flummoxed. She takes another swig and puts the glass down on the table. "I bet you did fine."

I shake my head.

"Well then," she says, "you'll just have to work harder."

I point at my maths book. "I'm trying."

I read the second trig problem again and again, express $\cos(3x) + \cos(7x)$ as a product... express $\cos(3x) + \cos(7x)$... until she leaves the room. She takes the bottle with her. I remember Olive asking once – did I think some mothers were born difficult? Or did something happen later to make them that way? At the time, it didn't cross my mind that she was looking for a serious answer. Olive's mum was difficult for sure. I couldn't imagine her ever being any other way. And okay so Mum drank sherry but it wasn't a problem yet. I still knew where I was with her. I could predict her moods.

I finish the trig and close my books. The background thrum from the fridge cuts out and suddenly the house is too quiet. Where is she? I go upstairs and find her on her bed, curled up like a baby, clutching her bottle. It looks like she's asleep until I go to draw the covers over her and her eyelids snap open. She stares up at me and I see her fury and her misery. My stomach starts to churn.

"Will Dad be home for dinner?"

"How would I know?" she says. "Your father tells me nothing any more." She closes her eyes. Shuts me out. But I don't need to ask what's wrong. It's almost seven o'clock now and he's still not home.

Back downstairs, I make toasted cheese and take it through to the living room, switch the telly on to *Tom and Jerry*. Tom brandishes a hammer and starts to nail Jerry's mouse hole shut. Thwack. Thwack. THWACK. He drives the last nail in but the racket doesn't stop. It takes another moment for me to register the knocking on the front door.

Two uniformed policemen are standing on the step. I recognise them straight away. Up close, the sergeant's taller than I thought this morning, and heftier. The constable still towers over him. He peers down at me through narrowing eyes and I lift my chin to him and refuse to shrink.

The sergeant says, "Are you Grace Balfour?"

I think about it for a moment before I say, "Uh-huh."

He says, "Can I speak to one of your parents?"

I shrug. "Dad's not home from work yet and my mum's in bed." The sergeant looks hard at me while the constable tilts his back head and examines the clear blue sky. It's still broad daylight. I know that's what they're thinking. I could tell them she's not well. It wouldn't be a lie exactly. She isn't fit to speak to them right now but they don't ask for an explanation.

The sergeant says, "When will your dad be home?"
I tell him I'm not sure.
He nods and says, "It's *you* we want to talk to. Nothing for you to worry about, you're not in any trouble, but we'll have to come back when your parents are present."

He takes a notebook from his breast pocket and, while he writes, the constable frowns down at me. He hasn't said a word so far and there doesn't seem much point to him being here except to make me feel small.

The sergeant rips a sheet out of the notebook and hands it to me. "Tell your mum and dad they can phone the station on this number to arrange a suitable time."

They turn to go. They still haven't said what they want to talk to me about, haven't mentioned Olive. And yet, the whole time they were on the doorstep, I had the weirdest feeling she was there as well, hovering above us somewhere, listening to it all. I suppose she thinks she's safe because I can't tell them where she is. But I could tell them stuff, if I wanted.

6

1969

It was summer term and the week Apollo 10 blasted off up to the moon to scout out the landing site for Apollo 11, the Sea of Tranquillity, a sea without a drop of water, a sea that made no waves. It was the week of Olive's twelfth birthday as well, and we were counting the days. When I went to the Broadfoots' door, she was still packing her school bag and her mum said to come in.

I looked at my feet. You had to take off your shoes when you went into their house and one of my socks had a hole in the toe. "It's okay. I'll just wait here."

"Please yourself, sweet pea." She turned and bawled up the stairs for Olive to get a move on then said to me, "She won't be long now, honeybun." She disappeared into the kitchen and left me standing on the step.

I never knew what she would call me next. Some days, I was teeny-bash. Some days, I was her pumpkin or her flower. She even had a pet name for that bit of me my own mum never mentioned. The night she let us have a sleepover, when it came time to wash and get into our pyjamas, she called through the bathroom door, "Don't forget your tooty fruities." I'd no idea what my tooty fruity was supposed to be till Olive pointed to the gusset of my knickers.

While I was on the doorstep, Peter dived into the hall and skidded full pelt back and forth across his mum's polished parquet floor in his stocking soles. His hair was not as red as Olive's, more of a strawberry blonde, and cut so short it bristled all over. He was in my class at school, but he never talked to me. He didn't talk to anybody much and the other kids called him Dumb Boy. That morning, he didn't say hello and I didn't expect him to. He wanted me to notice him though and every time he turned he checked to see if I was still watching. He went on and on like this till his mum came storming out of the kitchen.

"What have I told you?" She clipped his ear and said to me, "Olive won't be long now, cherub."

Peter was still holding his ear when Olive appeared. Her mum kissed both of us goodbye and said, "Take care, my petals." This gave me a cosy feeling until we were out of the square and Olive reminded me about the rules of kissing.

According to Olive, there were three kinds of kissing. The first kind was just Ordinary Kissing. These were the rules: Ordinary Kisses lasted one second or less and you got them or gave them but not both together. Usually, you got them on the cheek but you could get them other places as well. On the nose, for instance. You only got them on the nose if your mum or your dad was in a good mood. But you could get them on the cheek automatically – and we'd noticed they nearly always meant goodbye. Like when you went to school and when you went to bed.

That morning, Olive said her mum kissed everyone automatically and it didn't mean anything. She would kiss Peter too when he left for school and forget all about clipping his ear.

The second kind of kissing was Serious Kissing. These were the rules: a Serious Kiss lasted more than one second but less than ten. You could do it with your lips open or closed depending on how serious you were. It was supposed to mean I love you, and you shouldn't do it unless it was true because it was serious, but with married people it could get automatic and we'd noticed it usually meant hello. They did it in the kitchen when they got home from work and if they forgot there would be a bad atmosphere. You couldn't Seriously Kiss a friend, but you could practise with a mirror or the back of your hand.

We sometimes tried to imagine Seriously Kissing boys we knew, boys from school, but we always decided it was too disgusting. And Olive never mentioned Tony. The first I knew about him was the time he caught us breaking into the NAAFI, and I could tell right then she would take him seriously if he ever tried to kiss her.

The third kind of kissing was Cowboy Kissing. These were the rules: you did it with your mouth open and it lasted up to ninety seconds or as long as you could hold your breath. It was never automatic. If you kissed back you could call it French Kissing – but when you resisted it was a Cowboy Kiss. It happened in Westerns all the time, mainly in saloon bars and stables. The woman got insulted and the cowboy got his face slapped. If it happened in the saloon, he also got whisky flung in his face. Then he shoved her away and strode off through the swing doors laughing sarcastically. The main problems with Cowboy Kissing were running out of breath and falling in love. If you fell in love, it was THE END. This was why you had to resist.

That morning, on the way to school, she said we shouldn't trust any kind of kissing and especially not her mum's. It never meant what it was supposed to mean and we should never stop resisting. We went the usual way, down Springfield Road past the red phone box and across the railway bridge where someone had scrawled on the rusty wall:

YA BAS

DERRY OK

We sometimes wondered *who* Derry was, which one of the gang that hung around outside the snooker hall? We never thought to wonder *where*.

That morning, we waved to the signalman like we always did and, when we got to the end of the alley where her grandma lived, Olive stopped for a bit. She'd done this a few times lately. She never said what she was thinking, just stood there staring. The first house in the alley had wind chimes that tinkled in the slightest breeze, and I listened to them until she was done. Then we marched off the long way round by Station Road and down past the post office.

This was the last term we would walk to school together. After the summer holidays, she would take the bus north to the high school, setting out at eight in the morning and not returning till nearly five. Next winter, I wouldn't see her in daylight. I wondered if I would see her at all. High school was still months away for her but already she was worrying about who she would sit with on the bus. She'd made a list of five girls. Vanessa Reid was her top choice and Morag Ross was bottom. Vanessa was the latest girl in Olive's class. Since she showed up after the Easter holidays, all I ever heard was Vanessa this, Vanessa that. Vanessa had long dark wavy hair that rippled when she moved. Vanessa could do cartwheels and the splits. She lived on the new Meadow Estate, high on the rim of the town. There was a Meadow Road, a Meadow Avenue and a Meadow Way, but no meadow any more.

Past the school gates, Olive drifted off to join her classmates and I stopped and watched her getting smaller and smaller as she walked away. She was the only best friend I'd ever had.

*

In art class, I filled up my sky with overlapping clouds – silver, lead and iron. The substitute teacher was going round the class, peering over shoulders, and when she got to Peter she stopped and said, "What's this?"

Billy Cairns butted in, "It'll be another dinosaur, Miss. That's all he ever draws."

And the teacher spun round and said, "I don't recall asking you."

Everyone was watching now. She picked up Peter's picture. "What kind of dinosaur is it?"

Peter hung his head and started pulling on the ear his mum clipped that morning. You could see his hair bristling all the way down into the nape of his neck.

Billy said, "He doesn't speak, Miss."

The teacher glared and Peter's face went red. He went on staring at his desk until she put the drawing back.

When she got to me she said, "Where's the sun?"

I told her it wasn't out.

The substitute teacher was the second one that month. She didn't even try to remember our names. She just pointed and said *you*. There was a rumour going round that Miss Green, our regular teacher, was never coming back. Since the start of the school year, the class roll had gone up from thirty-five to forty-seven, and Miss Green ended up with so many children she didn't know what to do. Like the old woman who lived in a shoe, except Miss Green was only twenty-three and just out of teacher training college.

She'd rearranged our desks and chairs the modern way, in groups instead of rows, and let us talk among ourselves. At first, we weren't sure about this and we went on whispering. It took a couple of weeks for the racket to really get going. Then bit by bit we got wilder. Like the day we sneaked into the walk-in cupboard at the back of the classroom, one by one, until we couldn't fit another single body in. We'd waited to see how long it would take her to notice a pile of us were missing. She didn't notice though. The lunchtime bell went and we broke out, and she just blinked.

Billy Cairns took to wandering round the classroom, and Miss Green didn't even try to check him. Not until the day he crawled under her desk, and she jumped out of her chair and yelled at him to go and stand out in the corridor. But he kept opening the door, poking his head into the room and going, CUCKOO. And we all started laughing. No one meant to make her cry though. No one had wanted her to walk out and leave us.

*

At break I hung around with a new girl called Claire, who used to live in Devon before she moved to the Meadow

Estate. Claire didn't know what a play-piece was. I showed her mine, two chocolate digestive biscuits wrapped in tinfoil, and she said, "Oh, you mean tuck?" She had an apple. I felt sorry for her. I told her about the old school, about the asphalt playground and the spiky railing that separated girls' territory from boys', about the outside toilets with no roofs where green slime grew and spiders lurked.

The best thing about the new school was no more peeing in the rain. And for a while, we had all the space we needed, but the new houses kept going up and new pupils kept arriving, and it wasn't long until the main building couldn't hold us all any more. That year our classroom was in one of the prefabricated buildings we called the Huts. The walls of our hut creaked when the wind blew. Rain drummed down on the flat roof and drowned out the teacher's voice. Back in January, frozen fern patterns had decorated the inside of the windows and we'd been allowed to wear scarves and coats in class. Now in mid-May, we were baking with all the windows open.

Claire was wearing a new blue gingham dress, our summer uniform, and she looked crisp and cool. Mum hadn't had the time to take me shopping yet. I was squeezed into last year's dress and the seams under my armpits were digging in deeper and deeper as the day went on. It was a wonder I'd managed to get into it in the first place and I didn't know how I'd get it off again. By the time the afternoon bell rang, I'd given up thinking about anything else.

Olive was waiting for me at the school gates. Vanessa hadn't said yes. Vanessa hadn't said no. Vanessa couldn't decide who to sit with on the high-school bus. I started to tell her about Peter and the substitute teacher, and how she couldn't get an answer out of him, but Olive wasn't interested. All the way home, she was up one minute and down the next. Vanessa might still say yes... she might say no... she might... might not... I couldn't care less. The dress was biting too hard. I just wanted to get home. Find the scissors. Cut myself free.

7

1973

Three days since Olive went missing and still no word of her. The afternoon's sticky-hot and Jimmy Thompson's marching up and down the southbound platform with his coat buttoned up to the neck as usual. His face is broad and smooth from his chin up as far as his puzzled grey eyes, his forehead split by a deep V-shaped furrow.

We often see him at the station when a train's due. Mum says to me, "He likes to see who's waiting. Jimmy's interested in people in his own way."

We're standing in front of the ladies' toilet. The window's open wide, and the smell of pee makes my nostrils clench. Mum doesn't seem to mind the stink, but I'm worried any second now she'll notice where we are and start on about Olive again. How she could at least have left a note. She should've considered what not knowing where she is would do to Bill and Gina. How they would never get over losing Peter. And now this. The only decent excuse, as far as Mum's concerned, would be if Olive had some kind of accident. Or something worse. She never says what exactly. But she says maybe Olive only went into Stirling, or Glasgow, on a spending spree. Maybe she really meant to come home. Why else would she not take a change of underwear? Why else would the police be so involved? She is sixteen after all and, if she's dead set on leaving home, they can't force her back.

I still haven't got round to telling Mum the police were at our door last night and I put the sergeant's note under the clock on the mantelpiece. It's not like I've lied though, not like I hid it or anything. It's just, so far, I haven't mentioned it. If she looks, it's there for her to find.

Jimmy strides back towards us now and this time Mum

calls over, "It's a fine day, Jimmy. Are you not too hot in that coat?"

He comes right up to her and studies her face for a long minute, like she's a puzzle, and she smiles calmly back at him until he's got her solved. "You're not working later," he says. This is a statement, not a question. He knows her shift rota off by heart, but she answers anyway. "I've got the night off."

His eyes dart to me and he says, "Thirty-one-three-fifty-eight."

And Mum pretends to be surprised. "Grace's birthday – you remember."

"Of course," he says. He taps his head then turns and barks at the man next to us. "Harry Syme, two Beech Road, fourteen-five-forty-one."

The man salutes. "Yep, Jimmy, that's me."

He goes back to marching up and down. He used to be able to reel off the names, addresses and dates of birth of everyone who lived here, but that was before the developers came, before the town grew up and up the steep sides of the valley and smothered the high green fields. Jimmy still tries, but there's no way he can keep track of all the new faces. Today an unfamiliar woman is waiting for the train. Neat navy frock. Neat dark bob. He paces up and down the platform, slowing down to study her whenever he gets close. We can see that she bothers him, this newcomer with her private face and inward-looking eyes.

Now Jimmy's circling round her.

Now he stops in front of her and stares.

He demands her name, her address and date of birth. The woman's face is frozen – but we can guess what she must be thinking. Why should she give her personal information to this strange man?

"Except as far as he's concerned, she's the strange one," Mum says to me. "Jimmy's lived here all his days."

The train is pulling into the station, and the woman is

backing away. Mum tuts. "He's harmless. Can't she see?" But I'm not so sure. I can see the frustration boiling in his eyes.

We board the train and the woman takes the seat in front of us. Jimmy's alone on the platform. He strides up to the carriage window, peers in at her, and the woman gasps and shrinks back in her seat. The train starts to move, and I watch him getting smaller and smaller until he's a dot in the distance, and I wonder if he was there on the platform the morning Olive went missing. Her dad told us the ticket man couldn't remember serving a girl matching her description. Olive's hard to miss though: five foot ten in her stocking soles, never mind her cream patent heels, ginger hair, face smudged with freckles. Her dad thinks maybe she dodged her fare. He's so sure she got on a train. If Jimmy was there, he'd remember.

Mum leans forward and says to the woman, "It's only Jimmy. You'll get used to him." She explains she's a nurse, off-duty today, and we're going to Glasgow to buy our summer sandals then meet Dad from work.

"He doesn't know we're coming," she says. "We want to surprise him."

The woman smiles at this, and Mum tells her he's working overtime again this Saturday afternoon. He's been doing so much overtime lately it's getting to the point we hardly see him. So we're going to his office to show his boss he still has a family.

"You shouldn't have to," the woman says. She tells Mum her name is Sarah, and the two of them chat all the way to Queen Street Station. Sarah's husband is a sales rep, and they just recently moved into a bungalow in Meadow Drive. They've been trying for a baby for nearly two years now. Her husband says they still have plenty of time but Sarah cries every month. Mum has a way of getting information out of folk without them minding. They trust her when she tells them she works in the hospital. They shouldn't though. Nurses off-duty are no more reliable than anybody else. I haven't seen her at the sherry today but I can smell it mingled in with her perfume. Her irises are cloudy and her pupils are sharp little pinpricks. They stay that way even though we're sitting on the shady side of the carriage, even when the train enters the tunnel.

*

At Queen Street Station, Sarah says goodbye and heads out to the taxi rank. People scurry. People barge. Everybody wants to be somewhere else fast. Except for Mum, she doesn't seem to want to leave the station. She looks anxiously towards the exit, clutching her good tan handbag to her stomach. Before we go, she decides we need to check the train times home. In the booking office, we find a summer timetable and she stands there poring over it.

Finally she says, "I can't make head nor tail," and hands it to me.

She's been on the wrong page. I flick forward and read out the departure times after six o'clock. "But we're meeting Dad," I say. "He'll know all this already."

She snatches the timetable back. "We might not wait."

I sigh and rub the spot between my eyebrows. She's starting to drive me crazy. I thought the whole point of this expedition was to surprise him. We didn't need to come all the way to Glasgow for a pair of sandals. But her lips have set in a thin tight line and I decide I'd better not argue. We go looking for a kiosk and she buys Polo Mints and Kleenex. Then she goes to the public toilet and stays in there for ages.

While she's gone, I watch a gang of pigeons scrapping over a discarded hamburger near the exit. One of them is missing a foot. People scurry. People barge. No one sees you here. No one cares who you are. Not like home. I try to picture how it would've been if Olive got off here on Wednesday morning. Just one among the hundreds spilling on to the platform and flooding towards the barrier, she towers above the other women, red hair glinting, and still she feels invisible.

Mum comes back from the toilet with her perfume smelling stronger than ever. She pops a Polo Mint in her mouth and offers me the tube. I say, "No thanks," and glare at her. She's been drinking in the toilet again, and I want her to know that I know it. Her handbag's too neat to hold a whole bottle of sherry, but I worked out a while back that she pours it into cough medicine bottles, Benylin Expectorant, Actifed for a dry cough, easy to squeeze beneath her compact and purse.

*

The first shoe shop we try has the Doctor Scholl exercise sandals I want. They have moulded wooden soles and red leather straps and, as far as I'm concerned, there's no point looking any further. But she says we can't buy the first thing we see. We have to shop around. We have to trek all the way along Sauchiehall Street, weaving through the mobs of Saturday shoppers, in and out of every shoe shop. She makes me try on Scholl sandals with blue straps and Scholl sandals with cream straps. She says cream never clashes with your outfit, not like red. She buys herself a pair of navy slingbacks with kitten heels because navy goes with just about everything. Then she makes me try on clogs, which she seems to think are almost the same as Scholls. I have to tell her that they're not and she sighs and rolls her eyes at the shoe shop ceiling. Finally, in Timpsons at the far end of Sauchiehall Street, she agrees to Scholls with red straps and I get to leave the shoe shop with them on.

Dad's office is a fifteen-minute walk from Charing Cross down blackened sandstone streets towards the river Clyde. It's a quarter to five already and he's supposed to finish at five. We don't want to miss him and we're walking as fast as we can. Every so often, Mum rocks in her stiletto heels and curses the uneven pavement.

She says to me, "Folk live round here."

I stare up at the rows of windows, opaque with layers of

city grime, and wonder how they can breathe. I've got my old shoes in a carrier bag and, every second step, they bump against my thigh. The new wooden sandals are heavy on and trying to keep up with her is killing me. My calf muscles ache and blisters are ballooning on the pads of my heels and the soft undersides of my big toes, but I'd sooner suffer than take them off. I've wanted them so long.

It's just gone five to five when we arrive outside the Gordon Brothers' building. We still have time to go inside and show Dad's boss he has a family. But the doors are locked already. Mum presses the buzzer and, while we wait, I look up at the thick grey cobwebs clinging to the corners of the lintel.

I say to her, "The place looks dead."

She frowns and presses the buzzer again. This time she holds it down and we listen to it drilling through the Gordon Brothers' building, through the lobby, up the stairs, along the first-floor corridor and into the drawing office. Still no one comes – and she lets go of the buzzer and starts to knock. She knocks and knocks and knocks until I catch her arm.

"He's not here, Mum. They must've finished early."

She pulls away from me. "You don't believe that, do you?"

I don't know what I believe.

*

Back at Queen Street Station, there's half an hour to go till the next train home and Mum's not in the mood for standing around. We go into the station bar and she orders two black coffees and a double whisky neat. We find a table by the window so we can keep an eye on the departure board.

She says, "How's your feet?"

I tell her, "Fine." This isn't true, but she's not really interested anyway. It's just something to say. She stirs the whisky into her coffee and I turn away. For a while, we don't speak. I watch a daddy-long-legs dancing on the windowpane. I still haven't found the right moment to tell Mum the police are waiting for her call. It's been weighing on me more and more as the day wears on, and I keep wondering what makes them think I can tell them anything. It's not like me and Olive are friends any more. The daddy-long-legs reminds me of the cobwebs above the Gordon Brothers' door. This afternoon, I got the feeling no one had been in or out for weeks. But that can't be right. Dad goes there every day. I slip my sore feet out of my sandals and rest them on the cool tiled floor. I check the departure board, fourteen minutes still to go, and our platform number isn't showing yet.

And that is when I spot him, standing by the barrier with a thin blonde woman. She's carrying a blue guitar case, and he has his usual cigarette in one hand. His other hand rests in the small of the woman's narrow back. She isn't tall and when she speaks he bends his head towards her and smiles down. My dad. But I can't see him any more because my eyes are blurring up.

Mum says, "Your coffee's getting cold."

I blink and take a sip, make a face. "No sugar."

She looks over to the trolley where they keep the sugar sachets. "Bit late now," she says. "Let's just get out of here." She picks up her bag and rises from the table, starts to move towards the door.

I stay glued to my seat. I have to slow her down somehow. She mustn't see what I just saw. She turns to check what's keeping me and I say, "I need to put my old shoes on."

She tuts. "I thought you said your feet were fine."

I shake my head and lift my foot to let her see the blisters.

She says, "Well, hurry up then."

I fumble in the carrier bag and try to spin out the next few moments. But you can only take so long to change a pair of shoes, and soon we're out in the concourse, heading as straight as we can towards the barrier. People jostle. People barge. Mum tugs at my sleeve and points.

"Is that your dad? I think it is."

I stumble forward, and my heart is pumping so hard now I can hear the blood thudding in my ears. I look up just in time to see him striding through the barrier on to Platform 5. The thin blonde woman is watching him as well. Mum hurries on ahead of me and I can't tell if she saw them together or not. The woman is craning her neck, her hand up ready to wave, and I'm praying he won't turn and wave back, just keep walking away.

8

1969

That May before Olive went to high school, the new neighbour hadn't long moved in next door. Her name was June and her door was blue. She had long, pink, pointy fingernails and long blonde hair done up in a French roll, and she never went anywhere without her lipstick, not even to put out the bin. We'd never seen anyone like her before. Not in real life. Not in colour either, only black and white on the telly. It was hard not to stare. Olive didn't even try.

The new neighbour drove a two-tone grey Anglia and worked in Lizzie's hairdressing salon at the bottom of the high street. Most nights she had home clients on the side. We'd watch them make their way to her front door, heads down, roots showing. We saw them come out different women. We marvelled at bouffant flips and towering beehives rigid with lacquer. We hardly noticed the faces below. They'd hover on the doorstep and squint up at the sky. The least spit of rain and they delved into their bags, shaking out silk headsquares and unfurling umbrellas. If it wasn't raining, there would always be a row of towels pegged out on the new neighbour's washing line, peachy pink edged with satin ribbon.

One night after dinner, Olive knocked on her door and offered to bring in the towels. Olive could be annoying that way. She called it "being helpful". I called it "sucking up" and there was no way she was getting me to go to the door with her. I watched from my back garden though.

The new neighbour wasn't sure at first. She peered into Olive's face. "D'you live round here?"

"Across the square," Olive said. "I'm Grace's friend."

The new neighbour glanced over the fence at me, then

looked Olive up and down again. "My, you're tall for your age," she said. Like there was something wrong with that.

Olive's face went red and I called out, "She's older than me."

"Well, that explains it," the new neighbour said. She turned and went into her kitchen and came back with a clothes basket. "You can help too, Grace, if you like."

I just looked at her. Why would I want to?

*

Back then, Dad would always be home with me while Mum was on the night shift. He played the piano to keep himself company. Swing, Latin, boogie and blues – you name it and if I stayed awake long enough I got to hear it. Heavy on the bass. Fast and sweet on the roll. His foot pounding through it all, keeping time, until the steady thud and thud became the heartbeat of the house.

That night, he played "Take Five" while Mum got ready to go. She popped her head around my bedroom door as usual to say a quick goodnight. "And mind you don't disturb your dad."

She blew me a kiss and padded through to the bathroom for one last check in the mirror, and, after a minute, I heard her call out to him from the foot of the stairs, "I'm off now, love."

The front door slammed – and he let rip on what he'd been building up to for the past half hour. Rhythm and blues shook the walls, thumped up the stairs and through the ceiling. I picked a tuft out of the candlewick bedspread and dropped it on my pillow. It was peachy pink and fluffy like the new neighbour's towels. The music made me restless, made me want to get up and dance, but I was supposed to be in bed for the night. And Dad had sharp ears. He heard everything. One creak from me and he would bawl *GET BACK TO BED AND GET TO SLEEP.* Then he would begin again, the kind of tune that made my feet itch to kick off the sheets.

Those light May nights were the hardest to settle, nights when the darkness hid under the bed all squashed and sticky. He forgot the time. Forgot the neighbours. Not that he ever worried much about them. The new neighbour liked music, which was just as well. The last lot used to knock through the wall, but that didn't get them very far and when they came round to the door he said, "I'll do you a deal. You shut up your yappy dog and I'll pack it in." That Pekinese was a pest, according to my dad. He said the ankle-nippers were always the worst. All their yelping was pure frustration and they would rip your throat out quick as look at you if they were bigger. That's what they really wanted to do.

The new neighbour didn't have a dog. Or a husband. When she first moved in, Mum said she was a bit shallow but nice enough. At least, she didn't mind his noise. In fact, it turned out she loved his noise. She loved all kinds of music and, any chance she got, she hung over the fence and told him about it. Country, soul, rock and roll, even classical, she loved it all. And she went on and on. He couldn't get away from her.

Earlier that night, he'd come out to the garden while Olive was taking down the towels, and the new neighbour came out too. Yapping just as bad as the dog, if not worse – though I noticed he didn't complain about *her.* She told him she sometimes turned down the telly and listened to him play instead. Told him right in front of me and Olive. It was enough to make you sick in my opinion. Olive tried to tell me later it was meant to be a compliment. June was nice that way. She didn't see what my problem with June was. She said June's name a lot when she didn't have to, just to feel it in her mouth. But that woman was always sucking up to Dad. And Mum didn't think she was *nice enough* any more. *Far too damned nice* was what she said that night when he finally got away from her.

I picked another tuft out of the candlewick, and another, and another, made a long snaky line of them across the pillow. This used to help me settle down but it didn't work so well these days. I didn't stop though. If anything, I picked more and the bedspread got barer and barer. Pretty soon there would be no tufts left at all. I didn't know what I would do then.

I ran my fingers up and down between the furrows of what was left of the candlewick.

Up and down.

Up and down.

I studied all the little bones moving underneath my skin, blue veins swelling with the exercise. The new neighbour hadn't said anything about my playing when she was sucking up to Dad. Maybe she didn't like to mention it. Or maybe she just hadn't heard because I always practised with the soft pedal on. Mistakes didn't sound so bad that way.

The new neighbour was probably listening to him right now. I could picture her – sat there with the telly turned down, filing her nails and watching the man on the ten o'clock news, his lips moving but no words coming out. No bad news. Maybe she made up words of her own as he went along, pretended he was telling her how much he loved those pointy pink nails. And Dad would sound softer through the wall, but still close, as if he was there in the room beside her but playing with the soft pedal on, playing very softly just for her.

A long time ago when he still wore his hair slicked back, he used to work nights as well, in a jazz band called The Historians. Then I was born, and he had to choose between the band and the day job as a draughtsman at Gordon Brothers Engineering. According to Mum, it was no contest. "Family always came first with your dad," she said.

But that night, when he began to play slow and soulful, I could hear him dreaming aloud and, as I was drifting off, a change of rhythm jerked me awake and I heard wild waves of applause, the clapping of his secret audience. I got to hear them most nights now. Maybe the new neighbour heard them as well, maybe even joined in.

As the dark crept out from under the bed and slowly stretched to fill the room, I could hear him winding down. He played through a medley of old standards and I flicked tufts of candlewick on to the floor, one at a time, and tried to guess what was coming next. There was one tune he always played that made me think of Mum. Late at night, when she was away looking after other people, he played that tune to bring her home. Then his foot would go faster and the beat would grow urgent again. He played smoochy, romantic numbers for the new neighbour through the wall.

And his secret audience – they were always listening. They loved him. Everybody loved him. Me. And Mum. And the new neighbour as well, I could tell.

9

1973

The train's packed, seats all taken, people standing in the aisles. Everyone looks overheated. We push through carriage after carriage in search of Dad.

Mum says, "Excuse me."

"Excuse me."

"Excuse me."

The wooden sandals in the carrier bag keep knocking against my thigh. Finally, we spot him at the far end of the smoking carriage. Where else? We should've known. The carriage stinks like a giant ashtray, and Dad is staring into space as we wade through the fog towards him. I'm scared that he's thinking about the woman with the blue guitar case. I wonder if they've ever played together. We're almost up to him before he sees us and, for a second, he looks startled. Then his eyes light up the way they always do for Mum. He gets to his feet so she can sit.

He says, "You should've told me you were going to be in town. We could've eaten out for a change and got a later train."

Mum says nothing.

In the window seat next to her, a grey-faced man turns to the sports pages of his newspaper. And Dad says, "Marion?"

She glares at the headrest of the seat in front.

He says her name again.

Still nothing.

The grey man raises his newspaper higher and angles it to shut my parents out. I don't blame him. I'm embarrassed too. Five minutes out of Glasgow, the train stops and Mum gets up to let him out, and I wish I could escape along with him, follow him off the train and trail him through the tidy streets of Bishopbriggs.

"So can we afford to eat out still?" She spits this out at Dad before she sits down again. She shuffles over to the window seat and pulls me down next to her, leaving him to stand over us.

He says, "What's this about?"

"You know," she says.

He drops his cigarette end on the floor, grinds it out with his heel and lights another one. "But I don't know. Why don't you tell me?"

"This is not the place," she says. She turns her head to the window, lips shut tight.

Dad sighs and looks at me, and I read the question in his eyes. *Has she been drinking again?* I look away. He doesn't need to know. For once, I'm sure whose side I'm on. I gaze down at my hands and think about Olive's question: did I think some mothers were born difficult? I notice she didn't ask about fathers. Back then we were too young to see that dads could be part of the problem. The train stops at Croy, Lenzie, Larbert, Stirling and he's still on his feet though there are plenty of empty seats now. He chain-smokes for the rest of the journey, and we walk home in silence.

After the grey of Glasgow, the square looks like it's been coloured in by some primary school kid. Bright green grass and bright green hedges. Orange tiled roofs and chimney pots below a clear blue sky. Doors in red, yellow and blue. A police car is parked outside our house, and the sergeant and the constable from yesterday are plodding down our path. I turn to Mum and see her frown. I should've told her they'd been round before. I start to cringe, but Dad is smiling for some reason.

The far side of the square's still sunny but, on our side, the shadows are thick now. The sergeant calls Dad Brian, and Dad calls him Tommy. They start chatting at the garden gate, and it turns out they went to school together. I'm not sure yet if this is a good thing or not. Dad lights a cigarette and introduces me and Mum.

The constable remains anonymous. You can't forget he's there though. The way he hulks over us makes Dad look puny and Mum as dainty as a doll. I bet I could fit both my feet, with room to spare, inside one of his big black boots. He watches Dad closely while the sergeant talks. The way his grey eyes narrow makes me edgy, and I'm relieved that this time they're not directed at me.

The sergeant wants to know if Dad's still playing with the band. "The Historians, wasn't it?"

Dad gives him a sideways smile. "The band's history now, Tommy, split up years ago."

"I never got the jazz," the sergeant says. "Too clever for me, but you were good. Even I could tell that much. I can't believe you quit."

Dad shrugs. "What's this visit in aid of, Tommy?"

The sergeant dips his head towards me. "It's Grace we'd like a word with. I suppose she's told you we can't interview her on her own. As long as she's under sixteen, we need one of you present."

I don't know why but Dad just nods and acts as if I told him everything already. He says, "This isn't a great time, Tommy. What's so urgent you need to come out on a Saturday night?"

"We work all hours," the sergeant says. "Saturday night or Monday morning's much the same for us." His eyes shift to the Broadfoots' house across the square. "I can't say any more out here."

Dad turns to me, "Go on inside."

Mum comes with me, high heels clicking. The minute she gets through the door, she kicks off her shoes and pads through to the living room. She stands a bit back from the window, but near enough to keep an eye on them.

"So?" she says.

I think of all the other questions she could've asked. *What have you done now? When exactly did they speak to you? Were you planning to tell us, ever?* But she doesn't ask any of

50

those things. All she says is – *So?* The trickiest question of all, designed to make me say more than I want. I slip past her and lift the clock from the mantelpiece, hand over the note the sergeant gave me.

"You were in bed."

"Don't make this out to be my fault," she says, barely glancing at the note. "Why can't you just be open? It's the secrecy we worry about. We never know what you're thinking." As if she has no secrets of her own, as if there is no cough medicine bottle at the bottom of her handbag. She waits for me to say something and the silence stretches on and on till Dad comes in and tells us the police have gone for now.

"I told them it could wait. They'll be here at six on Monday. I'll try and get home early."

Mum says, "You better do more than try."

She turns away from him, looks out the window again and, for a minute, the three of us stand there saying nothing. I'm desperate to leave the room but I don't want to be the first to move and draw attention to myself. She's already got it into her head that I'm hiding something. In the end, Dad is the first to shift. He goes through to the kitchen and I hear him fill the kettle and strike a match to light another cigarette.

Mum says to me, "I'll speak to you tomorrow. I'm going to bed." She leaves the door to the hall wide open. Dad tramps back through the living room with a cup of coffee and follows her upstairs.

It's almost eight o'clock and my belly's rumbling but it doesn't look like there's much chance of any dinner tonight. I'm too tense to eat yet anyway, too tense even to sit. I turn on the telly to muffle the voices upstairs. I reckon they'll be up there a while. I go to the front window to check up on the Broadfoots' house and see if anything has changed.

Tonight I spot a little face peeping round the edge of the blue bedroom curtains, bristly strawberry blond hair gleaming in the last rays of the evening sun. And for a second, I think it's Peter and I'm so relieved to see him alive again that the weight of the last four years begins to fall away. It's not until he waves and sends me a cheeky grin that it dawns on me Peter never grinned like that, never showed his teeth, and this is Bobby.

I wave back at him and he ducks behind the curtain for a bit. Peeps out at me again. He must be four by now, getting big. But he was only a baby when Peter died, too young to remember a brother bigger than him. I wonder how much Bobby knows. Has anybody told him about Peter and his dinosaurs? Will Peter always seem to him more like a story than a real, live boy? And I wonder if Bobby is missing Olive yet. Is that why he's at the window now – watching out for her coming home?

Is that what I'm doing too?

10

1969

A family of snails inched up the garden path. Their soft damp bodies shrank and swelled beneath their shells. Three skinny trails of silver slime shimmered on the tarmac. At the far end of the path, a fresh hopscotch bed was chalked out ready for Olive to show up. It was neater than my usual efforts, no squint lines, no box smaller than the others. The lines were white, the even boxes numbered in red, odd ones in blue. In the starting box, the peever sat rough side up, looking like any old ordinary stone but secretly, underneath, it was slippery-smooth.

Olive was late, again. I hunkered down on the front doorstep to wait. It was still sunny on her side of the square but our stone step was cold and I'd soon have a stiff backside. Sometimes, it felt like I spent half my life on doorsteps, if not my own, then Olive's or some other one. The step was hardly ever an easy place to be. The bridge between inside and out. Between what folk liked to keep private and what you were allowed to know. The place you had to wait to be let in or be sent away. The place you sat and watched for folk.

Our house faced north and our doorstep was in permanent shade, unlike the Dark Side of the moon which wasn't dark half the time and its real name was the Far Side. That afternoon in art class, everyone had drawn a rocket except for Peter Broadfoot who drew another dinosaur. For days now in the playground, we'd been chanting the countdown all the way from ten down to... *Houston, we have lift-off*. Peter was the only one who didn't join in. He lived in another world from the rest of us, his own silent prehistoric planet.

I gazed across the square at the yellow door now, willing it to open. But it stayed shut. Olive had never been this late before. If she didn't hurry up there would be no time for hopscotch. The last few weeks, she'd started coming over to my place around five o'clock. To see me, she said, but I wasn't stupid. Really, it was so she could be near the new neighbour's house. We played hopscotch until June came home from work then Olive would rush off next door to collect the clothes basket and take in the towels.

Some nights, June was out of milk or tea or coffee and, after Olive brought in the towels, she would run round to the corner shop before the evening clients showed up. When she got back, June would say to keep the change and Olive never refused. Money was always good, but it was not the main thing. What she really wanted was for June to stop and chat. June didn't often have the time and Olive nearly always came away disappointed. But now and then, June would spare her a minute and tell her something new. Like the fact she was called after the month she was born. That's when Olive got the idea of changing her name to May. Her mum was having none of it though – and she said anyway, for it to be legal, you needed to make out a deed poll and you had to be sixteen for that. Olive said to me she could wait if she had to. She wasn't going to change her mind and, in the meantime, I could still call her May when we were alone.

I gave it a try. Just the once. It sounded stupid.

It was well past five now and June was back from work already. She parked her Anglia and stopped to speak to me on her way by. "All on your own today?" she said.

I just nodded. She could see for herself and there was nothing else to say.

She jingled her keys. "Hang the towels then. They can wait." She laughed and went inside.

I didn't like the way she laughed. The snails were drifting on the path, like three little sailboats on a big calm sea. I wondered who would get to me first, Olive or the snails. Pins and needles started pricking my legs and still I didn't move. Finally, the Broadfoots' front door opened and Olive skipped down the steps. She had on her favourite bell-bottom jeans and a pale blue sleeveless blouse gathered and knotted above her midriff. There was no way her mum would ever let her out like that, showing off her belly. She must have stopped behind the door and fixed the blouse at the last moment.

I got to my feet and waved but she wasn't looking my way. As she got closer, I could see the outline of her new training bra beneath the blouse. It was size 32 double A cup, the nearest to flat-chested you could get, but she claimed she needed it because she was developing. Her mind was always on her breasts these days. She complained they tingled all the time and they throbbed when she ran. One time up in Pisgah Wood, she took off her top to let me see what they looked like and the shape of them reminded me of two wee strawberry tarts. She said some girls in her class called theirs boobs, as if they were mistakes, but she refused to call them anything but breasts. That was their proper name and there was no shame in it. I thought there might be though. I'd never heard my mum say breasts except about roast chicken. My mum had a bust and she always talked about it as if it was one thing instead of two.

She turned the corner now, from her side of the square to mine, and I waved again. But still she didn't wave back. She looked down instead, undid the top button of her blouse and pulled the knot above her midriff tighter. And then, I couldn't believe it, she swanned on past my garden gate, smiling to herself. She didn't look round once, didn't even notice the new hopscotch bed.

I hunkered back down on the cold doorstep, made myself small. I was too embarrassed to wave any more, too embarrassed to call out her name, embarrassed to think how long I'd been waiting as if she was the only friend I had in the world. She turned in at the new neighbour's gate and the hedge was between us. I couldn't see her but I heard her rap on her door, the exact same rhythm she always rapped on my door. I always knew before I answered that it would be her.

The snails went on drifting.

The peever sat waiting.

I went to pick up it up, skirting past the snails on my way. Maybe they weren't a family after all, maybe not even friends. They probably didn't even know what a friend was. They just happened to be in the same place at the same time and decided to stick together for a while. Like me and Olive. I slipped the peever into my pocket and went indoors.

11

1973

All Saturday night and Sunday morning and into Sunday afternoon, Mum and Dad stay holed up in their bedroom. I have toast and beans for supper and toast and marmalade for breakfast. I have more toast for lunch and, when the bread runs out, I snack on cornflakes and digestive biscuits. Now and then their voices rise but never quite loud enough for me to make out what they're saying. The house is jangling with their tension.

Last night when Dad came downstairs to make more coffee, I pretended to be watching telly. This afternoon, I sit at the kitchen table and pretend I'm doing French homework. Since I saw him with that woman at the station, I can't bring myself to look at him. Yesterday at the barrier, I turned to see what she was like, and she had the thinnest eyebrows and small blue eyes, not as nice as Mum's which are sea-green and huge. I wonder if she knows about me and Mum. And does she know he smokes non-stop – in the bath, and when he's shaving, and at the dinner table between courses? Does she know he plays the piano with a cup of coffee on the lid and a cigarette burning down between his lips? And would she like him all the same?

The cigarettes are bought in bulk once a week and stashed in the kitchen cupboard nearest the back door, two cartons of two hundred Embassy Filters, and he never notices if the odd twenty-pack goes missing. It's almost three o'clock and I'm getting nowhere with the French translation. The words keep swimming. I leave my books on the kitchen table, tiptoe over to the cupboard and slip a pack of cigarettes up my sleeve.

Upstairs in my room, I go to open the window but I

can't light up. Half the square seems to be out there this afternoon, clipping hedges, cutting grass. Even June is out pulling weeds, gingerly, like they might bite. She has on a pair of green and cream gardening gloves and strappy sandals with sharp little heels that keep sinking into the grass. Across the square, Bill Broadfoot wheels his big black bicycle down the access path at the end of the terrace and climbs on. June straightens up and waves as he goes by, but he's hunched over the handlebars and doesn't seem to notice. She gazes after him for a moment then glances up at me, crooks a gloved finger and beckons me down. I decide I might as well. I suppose I'm a bit curious about what she wants – but mostly I'm just bored. I've been staring at the French for hours.

When I get outside, she says, "He's been off on that bike every day since Olive went missing. Cycles round all the parks. As if he's going to find her at the swings, she's a bit old for that. Where d'you think she went?"

Even if I knew, I wouldn't tell her, but she doesn't bother waiting for an answer.

"We missed her at Lizzie's on Saturday morning, had to do our own shampooing. Not what you want at your busiest time." She shakes her head and her hair stays strangely still. Hair-sprayed solid. "Then he comes into the salon," she says, "with a photograph of Olive, wants to show it to all the clients, starts asking if they've seen her. Betty Bruce was under the dryer and, of course, she couldn't hear him. So he starts shouting, and Lizzie made him leave. She felt bad about it, but the customers have to come first."

June pauses, tilts her head sideways and gives me a long look. "We're going to need a new girl. How would you like a wee Saturday job?"

I'm amazed she's asking me, thinks I'm capable. Not that I wouldn't like the money but I'm not good with people, not like Olive. I can't believe she doesn't know that. Plus it doesn't seem right to be giving Olive's job away so soon.

I say, "She might come back."

June shrugs. "She might, but Lizzie can't be doing with any more trouble."

She takes off the gardening gloves and examines her fingernails. They're painted a shimmering shade of cerise today. "You think about it. Let me know if you want the job and I'll put in a word for you."

I promise to let her know soon and go indoors feeling bad because I've already decided to take Olive's place.

*

It's gone six on Sunday evening before Mum and Dad are through. They're still up in their bedroom, and I've been staring at the ceiling for I don't know how long. This latest silence worries me more than any shouting. It feels too final and it's crazy how relieved I am when I hear their floor creaking.

Dad comes thumping down the stairs and says he's going out. "Make some toast and take a tray up to your mum."

I tell him the bread's all done and he says, "Improvise. I'll see you later."

He slams the front door so hard it sets the crystal vase humming. I go over to the windowsill and run the tip of my finger round the rim of the vase, keep it singing while I watch him stride out of the square. Bill Broadfoot cycles past on his way back home and Dad raises a hand to greet him, but Bill has his head down and doesn't seem to notice. He pedals past our house looking beat and, for a second, I start to feel sorry for him until I remember he never did notice what was going on around him. He should have though. Olive needed him to notice. Peter too.

I wander into the kitchen and heat a can of soup for Mum. It isn't much but, when I take it up to her, she shakes her head and tells me she has no appetite. The air's still hazy with Dad's smoke and the bedroom curtains are closed. I put the tray down on the bedside table and go to draw them back.

She says, "Leave them till I get dressed for work."

Her face is wan and I do my best to sound sympathetic. "D'you want me to run you a bath?"

She nods, gives me a weak but grateful smile. And I smile back like the decent daughter she wishes I was. In the bathroom, I stand and study my face in the mirror while the water runs. It's scary how many bits of her I can see. The same long droopy earlobes, velvety to touch. The same little mouth. Same indent in my chin. But not her big, green eyes. I have Dad's eyes, small and brown and secretive. I don't deserve her gratitude. I know I shouldn't encourage her to go to work tonight. I should be trying to stop her. She's not fit to be looking after other people, but the house is still jangling and it won't stop until she goes, and I'm prepared to do whatever it takes to help her out the door.

Down in the kitchen, I set up the ironing board and rummage through the laundry basket for one of her nursing tunics and a school skirt and shirt for me. I do her tunic first and take it back upstairs. She's in the bathroom now and I call out, "It's five past seven." This isn't true. I've added on ten minutes to make sure she gets a move on. Steam puffs through the seams of the door and I don't get an answer. In the bedroom, I drape the tunic over a chair. She has left the soup to go cold and I take the tray away.

The left cuff of my school shirt is missing a button and, when I've finished ironing, I get out the old Quality Street tin we use for a button box. On the lid's a picture of a soldier and a lady with a parasol, who looks a bit like Mum, chestnut curls and great big eyes. There's something smarmy about the soldier that reminds me of my godmother's husband, Geoff. He's lifting his hat to the lady and she's simpering back, falling for his smarm. I always think she needs a good rattling to wake her up and I shake the tin hard now before I open it.

There are all sorts here – fat leather buttons, silver ones embossed with anchors, wooden toggles from a duffel coat, ladybirds from my old dressing gown – all snipped off before we took our worn-out clothes to the ragman's van, in case they come in handy. Most of them have lived in the tin as far back as I can remember. They've never come in handy yet and I doubt they ever will. I dig out a plain white button and replace the lid, give the tin another good rattle and smirk at the thought of all the odd buttons jumbled up in the dark beneath the Quality Street couple.

Once I've fixed the shirt, I go back upstairs to check on Mum. She's still in the bathroom. At this rate, she'll be late for work. I rap on the door and call out that it's nearly half past seven.

She doesn't answer. All I hear is a tap trickling.

I knock again – louder – and still nothing.

And this is when I start to think something must be wrong. She's been in there too long. And why is she not answering? She could be dead for all I know. Fallen asleep and drowned. And I think I must want it to be true because the idea doesn't seem to worry me. I picture how her face would blur beneath the bathwater and still I feel okay. I try the door handle and I'm glad it's locked and there's nothing I can do to save her.

I sit down cross-legged on the floor with my back against the door, feeling weirdly calm. She'd better be drowned. It's the only decent excuse for this silence. I'm not sure what I should do next, so I sit for a while and gaze at the green swirls on the dark blue carpet, listen to my breath pushing out through my nose. The phone rings and I listen to that instead until it rings off. I gaze at a green swirl by my right foot and wonder who on earth dreamt up this carpet and why Mum chose it. The green's all right but the dark blue is grim. I think about yesterday afternoon, me and Mum outside Dad's office and how I had to stop her from battering down the door. Where was he then? Where is he right now when I need him? The phone starts again. It's probably the hospital wanting to know where she's got to and I don't know what I'm supposed to tell them. I go on staring at the swirl on the carpet and wait for the ringing to stop. Outside in the square, a car door thunks. June's television purrs through the wall. Behind the door, bathwater sloshes. This last noise takes a second to register.

Bathwater sloshes again. Gurgles down the plughole. And I'm not even slightly relieved.

12

1969

The new neighbour was the only woman in the square without a husband. She used to have one, according to Olive's mum, but he took up with a plainer woman. This woman was a widow and had two boys in high school. She had grey hair too. She didn't dye it. Olive's mum told us he probably preferred a natural-looking woman, and anyone could see that blonde came straight out of a bottle. Plus, she said, June was too vain to have a baby, or even a kiss, in case it mussed up her lipstick.

None of this stopped Olive's mum going to June's for a shampoo and set. It didn't stop my mum either. Her opinion of June was the same. She was still shallow and she sucked up to Dad, but her front room was a bargain, and half the price of Lizzie's salon. The first time June did her hair, Dad whistled when he saw her and told her she was looking good.

She said, "D'you really think so?" like she didn't believe him and went to the mirror to see for herself. She touched her hair and said maybe she would make it a regular thing.

She tried a chestnut tint next and then a demi-wave perm to give her hair a bit of body and, while she was at it, she made an appointment for June to cut my hair. They decided between themselves on a razor-cut pixie style. They didn't bother to ask what I thought. Razor cuts were the in-thing, according to my mum. And practical. It would save us both the trouble of untangling my hair every morning. No more comb tugging on knots. No more of my squirming and her yelping at me to hold still. Plus I could be more independent and wash my new short hair for myself. She didn't ask if I wanted to be independent. She just assumed. My hair was the only special thing about me, the only reason you would notice me. Not ordinary brown any more. It had grown darker over the years. Nearly black now, the colour of bitter chocolate, it fell straight to the middle of my back. I wasn't interested in practical hair and, anyway, it was part of me. I should've got a say.

The night of the appointment, Mum washed my hair over the kitchen sink to save June on time and hot water and I was sent next door with a towel wrapped round my head. June's lipstick matched her pink satin mules, and her hair was piled high and sticky with lacquer, like a swirl of blonde candyfloss. I had to stare. Her living room smelled of hairspray and singed hair. Trays of curlers, bobby pins and rollers were laid out on the sideboard, and behind the couch she had a hood hairdryer on a stand. The hood looked like a spaceman's helmet except that it was pink.

Between the couch and the television, an old kitchen chair stood on a large plastic sheet which was pink as well but pale and dirty-looking, like skin. This was where I had to sit, sideways to the television. The news was on with the sound turned down, just like I'd imagined, the newsreader's lips moving but no words coming out and, through the wall, Dad was playing Bach's "Air on the G String". Mum would be getting ready for the night shift about now. He always kept the music mellow until she went out.

June drew her steel comb through my hair and said, "Listen, it's the Hamlet cigar tune. I love that one, don't you?"

I tried to smile but it came out pained. I knew it shouldn't matter what she called it as long as she liked it. That's what Dad would've said anyway and, if it had been anyone but June, I might have agreed with him. But there was something about the way she said it I didn't like, the way she said everything, not just the Hamlet cigar tune. I felt her lift a hank of hair and pin it up. It wasn't like at Lizzie's where you could watch how you were changing in the mirror. In June's front room, you had to guess. I heard the snip, snip, snip of scissors, the razor shearing, the swish of hair dropping on the plastic sheet, felt my head getting lighter and lighter. I studied the wallpaper, trying to make sense of the cream and grey wavy pattern.

"Your friend was here earlier," she said,

She didn't need to tell me. I already knew.

June sighed. "She's very keen to help."

I knew that too. Olive was round almost every day to take in the towels.

"I wouldn't mind," she said, "but she's always waiting when I get home. I'd appreciate a minute to myself. Y'know what I'm saying?"

Of course I knew what she was saying. I had ears, didn't I?

"I suppose I'll have to tell her." She sighed again, deeper now, and her breath fluttered over my scalp.

Tell her what exactly, she didn't say.

"Her brother's a strange one though, not all there." She stopped snipping for a moment. Laughed. And this time her breath felt prickly.

"Does he ever speak?"

I said, "When he has to. Not just for the sake of it, like most folk."

She went quiet for a while. The scissors went on snipping till I felt cool air at the back of my neck. It was a strange, new sensation. Through the wall, Dad started to play "Somewhere" from *West Side Story*.

"Your dad sounds lonesome tonight," she said.

She didn't say lonely I noticed. "Lonesome" I felt wasn't quite the same thing. It sounded soppy, and I didn't like her talking about my dad that way. I told her "Somewhere" was his favourite song and mine too.

"You and your dad are close," she said. "Anyone can see."

I was glad *she* saw.

"You both must miss your mum," she said, "at night?"

I said yes, and this was partly true. Dad missed her for sure. Mostly I was in bed while Mum was at work. I didn't miss her much. June didn't speak again until she was done. She fetched a mirror from the sideboard and held it up in front of me. "There you are," she said.

But I couldn't see myself. The face looking out of the mirror was a boy's.

"Don't you like it? I think it suits you."

I glared at the boy in the mirror and said, "My back's itching."

She swept a soft brush over the nape of my neck. "Is that better?"

I couldn't bring myself to answer.

She said, "It might take you a wee while to get used to."

I stared down at the heaps of hair scattered on the dirty-pink plastic sheet. Then I got up and tramped right through it.

Back in our house, Dad was still at the piano. I dragged a stool through from the kitchen and climbed up to look in the mirror above the fireplace. The boy was there again. I stuck out my tongue to make sure he was me, and he stuck out his tongue back. It felt like June had made me disappear.

13

1973

Monday morning – and I'm halfway down the stairs when Dad slopes through the front door. He looks up and I stop dead, take in the rumpled shirt, the shadow of stubble on his jaw, his sorry eyes. I've never seen shame in his face before and I'm so embarrassed I have to look away. He didn't come home last night and, when Mum got out of the bath, she called in sick and crept back to bed.

He takes the stairs two at a time and wraps his arms around me, tells me everything will be okay. He'll make things right with Mum. The familiar smell of stale cigarette smoke half-reassures me but not enough to hug him back.

He says, "I'll be home early for the police."

I don't know why he can't be here all day. It's not like he has a job to go to. He doesn't have to keep pretending now. I mutter into his shoulder, "I don't need both of you with me."

He draws back a bit and scans my face. I guess he's thinking what I really mean is that I don't need *him*. He couldn't be more wrong. I hardly slept last night I was so scared he wouldn't be back and I'd be left with Mum.

He says, "Why didn't you tell us they were round before?"

I shrug. He wasn't there to tell, that's why, but I just say, "It's not like me and Olive are friends any more."

He ruffles my hair. "Did you fall out then?"

"Not lately, no."

I can't believe he hasn't noticed we stopped hanging around together years ago, but now is not the time to put him right. My belly's churning again and I can't face the school bus, can't face the same old questions from Claire about my weekend. But I don't want to stay here either. In this house. In this atmosphere.

I pull away from him and smooth down my hair. I say, "I

forgot my pencil case." This isn't true but I don't care. He lies too.

I scurry back up to my room and empty all the books and jotters out of my school bag, pile them in the bottom of the wardrobe. If Olive can do it, so can I, or at least I can disappear for the day. I stuff desert boots, a cheesecloth smock and my favourite, red brushed-denim jeans into the bag, dash back downstairs and slam the front door behind me. No goodbye to Dad.

In the middle of the square, the patch of grass is slick with dew and light catches on fragile cobwebs slung between the rose bushes. It's almost five past eight as I pass the Broadfoots' gate and hear their Hoover humming. Gina Broadfoot never stops. Even the day after Peter died, we spotted her washing the windows. Mum said to me she couldn't help herself. Cleaning was Gina's way of coping and she needed to cope somehow.

I take the route Olive took the day she disappeared: a right turn at the corner, through the lane with no name, past the Dobsons' white rabbits in their lettuce-strewn hutch, follow in her footsteps down Springfield Road as far as the phone box. Inside it stinks of beer and pee and cigarettes and I use my school bag to wedge the door open and let in some fresh air. The receiver is sticky from greasy fingers and spittle. I hold it a bit away from my ear and listen to the dialling tone, pretend to make a call while the convoy of buses starts rolling by on the way north to school. The phone box windows are so grimy I can't tell one bus from another and I can't see if Claire is there in our usual seat or not.

*

Down at the station, I bypass the ticket office and slip in the side entrance straight on to the southbound platform. The Glasgow commuters have already left, without Dad today. He promised he would talk to Mum and make things right, but it's not only up to him, and I'm not sure she'll listen, not now, not after him staying out all night. Between me and the ladies' toilet, a bunch of office types and shop assistants are waiting for the train to Stirling, six miles down the track. Nobody could remember seeing Olive on the platform the morning she left, her dad said. Today some have their heads in newspapers. The rest seem half-asleep, staring into space, and I slink by them like a ghost.

The ladies' toilet has just been sluiced and the floor is sopping wet. In the cubicle, the bleach fumes are so strong they catch at my throat and make me cough. I balance my bag on the cistern, change my top half first and step out of my school skirt. The next bit is trickier: how to get into the jeans without soaking the hems or my feet. I try it standing. Wobble. I try it sitting on the loo. Outside a train arrives and departs and I give up, drag on the jeans and tie my bootlaces.

Before I leave, I check out the wire mesh waste bin where Olive hid her school bag. Stowed or ditched, her parents aren't sure which. Only I know she was planning to take off. I could've told them that much. They could've stopped worrying about her being dead at least. But then they might have asked what else I knew and I would've had to lie. In any case, even if I told them everything it wouldn't help them find her.

I sling my bag over my shoulder and go back to the platform, and the smell of bleach comes along with me. Both north and southbound platforms are deserted now. I sit on the nearest bench and, for a while, I'm the only one waiting. Not that I can afford to take a train anywhere, and I'm already wishing I hadn't skipped breakfast. The pittance in my pocket won't buy me much to eat. I start to wonder how long it took Olive to save up sixty-five pounds and how long she can manage to make it last. And I wonder if June was serious about me starting at Lizzie's and what I could do with sixty-five pounds.

The ticket man comes out of the office wielding a long pole with a spike on the end and asks what train I'm waiting for. I smile back all innocence and tell him the next one. This is not a lie exactly. Waiting for the next one doesn't mean I have to get on it.

He gives me a funny look. "It'll be another forty minutes."

And I nod as if I know already.

He hops down on to the track and starts spearing litter. Every now and then, I catch him glancing up at me. His eyes are dark and shrewd. You can tell he doesn't miss much and yet he told Olive's dad he didn't remember her buying a ticket, and Olive is unmissable. A fat man lumbers on to the northbound platform lugging a large brown suitcase and stops opposite me across the track. His feet look too small to support him and, when he lets the case drop, I half expect him to keel over but he just checks his watch.

Down on the track, the stationmaster goes on spearing litter and transferring it into a tattered sack. If I hang around much longer, he'll be back asking questions. I'm trying to decide where to go next and what I can afford to buy for lunch when Jimmy Thompson shows up. He marches to the north end of the platform and marches south again, clutching a rolled-up newspaper to his chest. His other hand slices back and forth, back and forth, like a clockwork soldier. Every time he passes, his eyes flick to me and he picks up a bit more speed until his forehead starts to bulge either side of his V-shaped frown. By the time the stationmaster looks up, he seems about ready to burst.

"Morning, Jimmy, you're late today."

Jimmy stops dead and the ticket man smiles.

Jimmy doesn't smile back. Jimmy doesn't do friendly. Jimmy does numbers. He waves the rolled-up newspaper and barks, "Six critical signal errors in the last three months."

The ticket man grins. "Is that right, Jimmy?"

Jimmy points up the track towards the signal box. "Six at this junction."

The fat man looks to where Jimmy's pointing and the ticket man's grin gets broader. "Are you sure it wasn't five – or seven maybe?"

"Six," Jimmy says.

"Aye well, if you say so, six will be right. You never get the numbers wrong."

Jimmy gives him a curt nod and goes back to pacing up and down.

I want to ask him about Olive. If Jimmy saw her get on a train, he'd remember and the exact time as well, but I'm scared to come between him and his marching. The ticket man climbs back on to the platform and takes the pole inside. The next time Jimmy passes, I wait for him to glance my way, ready with a smile. He seems not to know how to take it and his marching gets jerkier.

The Aberdeen train pulls in and when it departs the fat man is gone. A minute later, the ticket man is back, with a broom this time. He goes to the far end of the platform and starts sweeping towards me, and I decide it's time make a move. I pick up my bag and, as I get to my feet, Jimmy draws level with me again.

This time he stops, and a bunch of numbers fly out of his mouth so fast they all run together. "Twentyfour fivefiftyseventhirtyonethreefiftyeight WHY do girls not go to school?" His eyes are boiling.

And I say, "What?"

He starts again, snapping the numbers out one at a time now. "Twenty-four-five-fifty-seven-thirty-one-three-fifty-eight."

For a second, I still don't get it. Then it clicks. "You mean Olive and me, our dates of birth, why do we not go to school?"

Jimmy nods. "Twenty-four-five-fifty-seven."

I smile and nod back. "Yeah, that's Olive. Did you see which train she got on? Last Wednesday? The nineteenth?"

He jabs his thumb towards the exit.

I can't make up my mind if he wants me to leave now, or if he's trying to tell me Olive didn't get on a train. "She left the station, is that what you're saying?" I want to be sure, but Jimmy's eyes have glazed over.

I try again. "D'you know where she went?"

He waves his rolled-up newspaper at me and says, "Six critical errors in three months at this junction."

I say, "That's a lot of mistakes. Were there any last week? What about the nineteenth?" But I can see from the way he gazes through me there's no chance of getting his attention back.

I head for the exit and try to think where Olive might have gone next. There's a bus stop next to the station but the buses only go as far as Stirling, which isn't very far at all or big enough to lose yourself. You'd have to be daft to run away to Stirling. At the top end of Station Road, there's the main road from Aberdeen to Glasgow. Thundering heavy goods vehicles and whizzing sales reps' cars, all on their way to somewhere more important. Maybe Olive decided to save money on fares and hitch a lift instead. But hitching is risky round here. The wrong car might stop, a driver not just passing through, and not an incomer either, one of the old-town locals who knows exactly who you are, knows who your parents are, grandparents too, and won't take you anywhere but home.

I head around the corner into the alley, into the shadows, into the chill. I almost never come this way even though it's quicker. But twice in the last week, I've let the alley draw me in. I don't suppose I'll ever know all there is to know, but I know this much: it all started here, the reasons Olive wanted to disappear.

Goose pimples prickle my arms as I pass her grandma's house. Behind the dusty nets, heavier curtains are still drawn, upstairs and down, and a lone milk bottle stands on the doorstep. It's almost ten o'clock and the milk doesn't seem quite right. She should've taken it in by now. Old women don't lie late. When I get to the bottom end of the alley, I waver for a moment then turn and dart back to the doorstep. Lift the milk. I'm not keen on milk unless it's chilled but my mouth is dry. I'll need something to drink soon and this is free. I walk away briskly, guilt tingling my skin.

14

1969

On Olive's twelfth birthday, I gave her a troll with electric blue hair, and we stood at the living room window looking out for her grandma. She hadn't been invited, but Olive said that wouldn't stop her coming. Her grandma never missed a birthday. Peter was in the back garden playing with his army of plastic dinosaurs, and the baby was upstairs in his cot. Olive's mum came through to tell us he needed his sleep and to keep the noise down though we weren't making any. We were trying to decide if the troll was a boy or a girl, and Olive asked what her mum thought.

But she just said, "Don't stand so close to the window. You're steaming up the glass."

She disappeared through to the kitchen and Olive whispered in my ear, "She wishes I didn't breathe at all."

We laughed and blew as hard as we could, made big misty clouds on the windowpane then ran outside to wait on the front doorstep till her grandma came. We bumped into Olive's grandma sometimes, coming out of the Co-op butcher's at the top of the high street, and every single time she told us she was having sausages for tea. Sausages were all she seemed to eat, but she would have to do without sausages today. We were only having cake and sandwiches, Olive said. She divided the troll's hair into three sections and wove them into a braid. We decided it wasn't just a boy or just a girl. It was a bit of both.

"A goy," Olive said.

I said, "A birl."

The troll's face somehow managed to be happy and fierce at the same time, and Olive said it was the best way to be. Fiercely happy. Happily fierce.

Her grandma finally appeared at the far corner of the

square, lugging the red-and-green tartan shopping bag she took wherever she went. I always got the feeling there was something in it she couldn't leave at home, something she had to guard. Though what this might be, I had no idea.

We ran to meet her and walked her back to the yellow door, and Olive said to come in. But her grandma shook her head and stopped on the step.

"I'll wait. You go and tell your mum I'm here."

She made me wait with her. We stood and peered into the hall together, breathing in the lavender and beeswax polish wafting up from the parquet floor and, after a while, she turned and looked at me. "What happened to all your lovely hair?"

I bit my lip and didn't even try to answer. There were no words for how it felt to look like a boy.

She said, "Never mind, you can always grow it back."

I decided she was all right then. At least, she didn't try and pretend it suited me.

Olive's grandma looked like a squashed-down, crumpled version of Olive's mum. Shorter, fatter and more wrinkled. She wore her silver hair in a loose bun low on the nape of her neck. While we were waiting on the doorstep, she told me her hair used to be as red as Olive's and she'd never had it cut, never in her life, and when she let it down it was long enough to sit on.

I asked if it was heavy and how many pins it took to keep the bun in place.

She said, "Pins – I never have enough. But you get used to the weight. I wouldn't want to be without it. I might get strange ideas." She winked at me and peered through the doorway. "I suppose we'll have to take our shoes off."

I said yes.

She heaved a sigh and a silvery wisp of hair escaped from the bun, soft and wild. She was nothing like my grandmas. They both had short and neat permed hair and never waited on the doorstep. Gran Balfour never even knocked, just opened the door and walked straight in. She'd call out – *it's only me* – and as soon as I heard her voice I always felt safer somehow, even though I hadn't noticed I wasn't feeling safe before.

Olive's mum came bustling into the hall now. "You better come in," she said. No smile and no hello.

"You too, Grace, shoes off."

We padded into the living room and Olive's grandma said, "All changed again I see. Is that a new sideboard? What was wrong with the one you had?"

Olive's mum said, "You get sick of looking at the same old things."

Her grandma shook her head and another wisp of hair escaped from her bun and floated by her ear. She delved into the tartan bag and brought out a parcel and card for Olive. The card had a pound note inside and three crosses for kisses. We already knew what was in the parcel. Every year for Olive's birthday, her grandma knitted her a new cardigan.

The latest one was a barely there shade of pink. "Oyster pink," her grandma told us while Olive tried it on.

The buttons were imitation mother of pearl, shaped like shells, and her grandma bent to fasten them, starting from the bottom and working her way up till they were face to face and she smiled into Olive's eyes. "It's bonnie on," she said and placed her hands on Olive's shoulders, turned her round to face her mum. "Gina, what d'you think?"

She stroked Olive's hair while she waited for an answer. The silence went on and on till in the end she said, "Well?"

And Olive's mum said, "Nice."

Olive and her grandma sat down close together on the couch now and her mum perched on the edge of the fireside chair. No one said where I should sit. I stayed behind the couch out of the way. I didn't know any other families apart from my own, not like this, not how they were inside. I wished I wasn't there.

76

Olive asked her grandma how long it took to knit the birthday cardigan, and her grandma said three days. "I used to knit all your mum's woollies, pullovers and cardigans, mittens and tammies, even a coat once. Remember the damson coat, Gina? The cable-knit? It took me weeks."

"I don't know about damson," Olive's mum said. "More like maroon." She frowned in my direction and I looked away towards the door.

"Right," she said and clapped her hands, "Time for birthday cake. Take the cardigan off now, pet. It's not machine washable and we don't want it getting stained."

Olive got to her feet and started to undo the buttons, slowly, like she didn't want to. She handed it over and her mum folded it up and put it in the top drawer of the sideboard. Then Olive turned and looked at me. We both knew she wouldn't see the cardigan again. Her mum would make it vanish, the same as all the other birthday cardigans. She didn't like hand-knitted things. She'd rather have shop-bought machine knits, preferably from Marks & Spencer's. Next time the ragman came round, she would take the cardigan out to his battered van, like she did every year, with a bundle of old clothes and the garden shears. For the old clothes, the ragman would sharpen the shears. And for the latest birthday cardigan, she'd take two balloons on sticks, a pink one for Olive and a blue one for Peter. Peter always burst his first.

Before we cut the cake, we had to get him in from the back garden and, when he saw his grandma, he went racing up to her with a big rush of questions, the most I ever heard him say. Could he sit next to her at the table? What was in her bag? Why did she only visit on birthdays? His grandma was about to answer when his mum butted in and sent him to wash his hands. He stamped upstairs to the bathroom and, seconds later, he stamped down again. It wasn't nearly long enough. His mum took one look at his hands and sent him straight back. By the time he finally got to sit, he'd changed back to his usual dumb self. His grandma asked what he'd done at school that day and he just hung his head.

The cake had pale pink icing with dark pink roses, and Olive asked if we could help put the candles on but her mum hadn't bought any. "They're messy anyway," she said. "Plus the wax stinks when you blow them out."

Olive's grandma shook her head. "But the lass needs candles to make her birthday wish."

And Olive said, "It's okay."

It wasn't okay though. She hung her head as well now and sat down next to her grandma at the table. No one said where I should sit. I had to wait till her mum sat and there was only one chair left.

15

1973

No rain for days and the river is low. I pick my way across bone-dry boulders and on to the island in seconds. It shouldn't be this easy. No danger of slipping – but danger was always the point. I've never been here without Olive before. There are loads of places I've stopped going in the last four years, all the wild and lonely places. I realise now I've missed them, missed the dens and adventures, the freedom and the fear. Missed her, I suppose.

I stand the milk bottle in the river to keep it cool and park myself on a rock facing upstream. I untie my desert boots and peel off my socks. I had just enough money for a Mars Bar and a small packet of salted peanuts, and I tear open the nuts now. I have hours still to kill and nowhere to go, nothing to do except think.

Clouds of wispy insects are dancing just above the surface of the water, wings almost transparent in the sunlight. I dip my feet through them, and the river keeps coming and coming towards me. It comes in lots of different streams, fast and slow, broad and narrow, splitting, joining up again. I close my eyes and let it all wash through me, let it sweep my thoughts away to the sea.

Is Mum listening to Dad yet? Will she give him a chance?

I don't like milk unless it's chilled.

And I'm a thief.

But guilt can feel good, make your skin tingle.

And if Olive's really gone – gone forever – maybe I can start over as well, maybe even quit taking Dad's cigarettes, make the packet in my bag the last.

I open my eyes now and the river keeps coming, flowing around me, flowing through me. Upstream where the bank is steep and the water is squeezed narrow and fast, I spot something dangling from an overhanging tree. At first, I can't make out what it is, the way it's slung over the branch by its hind legs, body stretched out long and skinny, front legs pointing down. Like it's ready to dive clean out of the coat hanging off its bones. Grimy grey wool. A dead lamb. It must've been up there a while, long enough to be riddled with maggots, and it didn't get there on its own. Somebody hung it, deliberately. Some weirdo. I can't think of any good reasons.

The salted peanuts are making me thirsty but I can't stomach the milk now. I light a cigarette instead. Try not to look at the lamb. Try listening to the river again. But I can't shake off this queasy feeling. It serves me right for stealing – even though the bottle was asking to be taken. I should've knocked on the door and made sure Olive's grandma was okay. Old women don't lie in bed late and leave the milk out to go sour.

*

Back in the station toilet, the floor has dried and the smell of bleach has faded. Outside, the platforms are deserted. No one saw me coming in. I change back into my school uniform, bundle the jeans and cheesecloth top into my bag and inspect myself in the mirror above the sink. Hair sticking out at weird angles, my shirt and skirt a crumpled mess. I splash cold water on my face, run a comb through my hair and tuck the ends behind my ears. But it's too early to go home yet. The school buses aren't due to roll back into town for another ten minutes.

I light a cigarette and stand by the open window blowing smoke out on to the southbound platform. When I looked on my way back, Olive's grandma still hadn't opened her curtains. I'm not sure what it means, maybe nothing, but I think I'll check again tomorrow. I've already decided to skip school again and take a packed lunch up to Pisgah Wood. It's four years since I was last up there. It's not the sort of place you go alone. But we always loved the velvety moss, the cool shade, the hush. We knew all the best trees for climbing and Pisgah's secret paths and hidden clearings. Not that I really expect to find Olive there, but still I need to look. I won't relax until I'm sure.

I flick the cigarette end out of the window, rinse my hands and try to smooth the creases from my skirt with damp palms. It makes no difference. I'll have to walk home in this state and hope nobody sees me, nobody that's interested at least.

But there is always somebody.

I open the door and walk straight into the ticket man. He points down at the cigarette end still smouldering on the platform. "Is this yours? The toilet is for passengers. Do you have a ticket?" His eyes drill through me. "Well, do you?"

I shrug and blush. He doesn't need to ask. He already knows I don't.

He grinds out the cigarette with his heel. "I know your parents. I know exactly who you are. Don't let me catch you here again."

*

Dad's not around when I get home and Mum's in the kitchen and, for a minute, everything seems back to normal. Floor swept. Beef stew simmering on the cooker. She looks me up and down, taking in my crumpled state, and I wait for her to say something, but she just empties a bag of potatoes into a basin of water, starts to peel. Sometimes her silence feels worse than yelling. I want to ask where Dad is now. I want to know what she's decided. Is he forgiven? She doesn't make it easy though. She keeps peeling and dropping potatoes into a pan of cold water as if she's forgotten I'm even here.

I go through to the piano and start my practice. Arpeggios. Crashing up and down the keyboard. I don't care if the whole square hears, bum notes and all. The police are due any minute and Dad's still not home. He promised he'd be early. Not that him being here will make any difference.

There's nothing I want to tell them about Olive. Nothing they can make me say. I thunder up and down the keyboard till Mum bursts through the door.

She says, "That's enough."

I turn and look at her, and my fingers keep moving, cling on to the pattern, up and down, up and down. She starts to cry now, glares at me through dripping tears, and still I go on playing. All she can see is my defiance and I can't explain, can't find the words to tell her it's not just that.

She retreats upstairs to her bedroom and I switch from arpeggios to tonic scales and more mindless repetition, keep going until my fingers ache. Then I get up and check the window in the hope Dad will be striding into the square, loosening his tie the way he always does when home's in sight. Instead I see June on her way back from work. She waves and sends me a pink lipsticky smile. And the ginger cat is here again, prowling past the Broadfoots' gate this time.

Mum has abandoned the stew and now I smell it burning, dash through to the kitchen to find the meat sticking to the bottom of the pan. I snatch it off the hotplate and add a bit of water but it's too far gone to be rescued. I start to worry that she took the sherry bottle upstairs. I need her to be sober for the police. I search the sideboard, search all the kitchen cupboards. No sign of it anywhere.

I spot her handbag under the kitchen table, pull out the Benylin bottle and hold it up to the light. Empty. I dig into the bag again and find a smaller bottle. *Valium 2mg (to be taken twice daily)*. Almost empty too, but the date on the label says she got it on Friday, only three days ago. I tip what's left into my palm and count them back into the bottle. This is not the first time I've had to check. I know what she does. She should've taken six but twenty-four are missing. Not enough to kill her. It never is. Just enough to kill the pain of being her a while. I wonder when she took them. She hasn't had much chance – most likely in the bath last night after he went out.

I'm still holding the bottle when Dad walks through the door. He drops his evening paper on the kitchen table, says, "Where is she?"

I tell him she's in bed and the dinner's burnt, and he glances at the pot and sighs. "How's she been?"

I show him the Valium bottle and try to explain what I just worked out. I say, "She could've fallen asleep and drowned."

His jaw tightens and, for a minute, we stare at each other until he snaps, "It's none of your business. Put it back where you found it."

16

1969

The morning after Olive's twelfth birthday, the troll was peeping out of her blazer pocket. She'd undone the braids and backcombed its blue hair so it stood on end and it looked fierce.

"Like the mood I'm in," she said.

She raced ahead of me across the railway bridge. We were late for school. She didn't run so fast these days now that she had breasts but she was still faster than me and I was used to running after her. It didn't mean I liked it though. I got tired of trying to keep up with her. Sometimes, I thought a slower friend would suit me better, someone like Claire who didn't rush about, someone I could beat for a change.

At the far end of the bridge, she turned and shouted back, "Come on."

When I caught up, she grabbed my hand and tugged me towards the mouth of the alley. She didn't say why, but it wasn't just because we were late. We were nearly always late and we still went the long way round. I told her no and pulled against her. I told her over my dead body. We both knew she wasn't meant to go near her grandma's house. I dug my heels into the ground.

But she was bigger and she pulled harder and I couldn't hold her back for long. We jolted and we lurched. Then we were belting through the alley, faster and faster, till the soles of my feet were stinging. I yelled at her to slow down, let go my hand, but she wasn't listening. At the bottom of the alley, she swerved left and charged across the road bridge, dragging me along behind her. We were halfway up the high street before she finally let go. Both of us were panting and Olive was grinning.

She said, "I've done it," and her grin seemed bigger than

her face, the biggest grin I ever saw. She grinned all the way to school. She'd gone in the alley and nothing terrible had happened.

*

That afternoon, I was at the school gates early, watching out for her among the mob of kids shoving through the main door. The air was muggy, the sky heavy and threatening to rain. I spotted Vanessa Reid first, still looking crisp at the end of the day in her gingham dress – and right behind her a rumpled Olive. I knew she was still hoping Vanessa would choose her to sit with on the high-school bus. I thought she should have more pride and quit following Vanessa around, ask someone else to sit with her instead, someone who at least would give her a straight yes or no. I watched Vanessa glance back at her and toss her hair so it rippled. It was obvious she knew she was the pretty one.

She didn't wait for Olive. She darted forward and tapped Patsy Pringle on the shoulder and they skipped off together giggling and left Olive trailing. They skipped past me and I glared straight into their giggling faces but they took no notice. I glared at Olive next. She didn't notice either, didn't even look at me. She was too busy gazing after them. A blue car drove up and stopped a bit ahead of them, and they ran to catch up, jumped in the back, and the car purred off down the empty road and vanished round the corner.

The pavement was heaving with kids. We dodged a bunch of jostling boys and Olive said to me, "I wish we didn't have to walk."

I told her I didn't mind and she said, "Well, you should. Walking makes us look poor."

I said, "Since when?" She didn't need to tell me though. I already knew. "We didn't look poor till Vanessa got here."

Olive said, "You're jealous."

And I said, "What of?"

But she just nodded. "Yes, you are."

We didn't speak again all the way down the high street. I'd never thought that I was poor before Olive put the idea in my head. Poor meant you were starving, thirsty, homeless, naked, cold, and I was none of these things. But I was poorer than Vanessa now, poorer than Patsy too, and it didn't matter that just about everyone walked home the same as me. I looked down at my shoes and I saw poor scuffed toes, and my socks weren't as white as they should be either, and I had to wear my winter skirt because my gingham dress didn't fit. But none of this meant I was jealous. I still had more pride than Olive.

We got to the bottom end of the alley and she stopped and looked at me. "So are you speaking yet?"

I just shrugged. I felt too poor for words, but she took it as a yes. There was something bold and spikey about her eyes all of a sudden – and jittery as well. She said she wanted to go in the alley again, try and find her grandma's house this time. She claimed she didn't know which house it was, claimed she'd never even visited. I wasn't sure I believed her. Okay, she wasn't allowed to go there on her own. But everyone went to see their grandma, didn't they? On Sundays? With their mum and dad?

Thick charcoal clouds were rolling over the slate roofs as we started up the alley. We zigzagged from side to side checking the nameplates on the front doors, looking for Dolinsky. Olive said this was her grandfather's name. She claimed she'd never met him and she didn't want to. All she knew about him was he came from the Ukraine and he had no time for anyone.

I said, "You mean he's alive?"

And she said, "Uh-huh."

This was news to me. From the way she talked, I always got the idea her grandma lived alone. Plus there was never any *love from grandpa* on her birthday cards. I thought she must be kidding me and she just made him up. Why else would she not have told me about him before?

Olive shrugged. "There's nothing to tell. I don't even know him."

I thought about her aunt Sandra and cousin Frank in Canada. Olive had never met them either but she told me loads about them. She thought because they lived abroad that automatically made them interesting. It didn't though.

I said, "What about your grandma then?"

"What about her?"

"You know *her*. You've *met* your grandma."

Olive said, "Yeah, but she has to come to our house. We never go to hers."

I thought that was weird. "So where's the Ukraine anyway?"

She said it was behind the Iron Curtain, and I pictured a massive sheet of cold dark metal, miles and miles wide, with no way round and no way over. I wanted to know how her grandpa managed to escape but she had no idea except it must've been before her mum and her aunt Sandra were born, maybe to do with the War.

We found the house halfway up on the dark side of the alley where the cottages were more cramped together. The front of the house was narrow with a single window downstairs and one above. The door was painted black and the brass nameplate had DOLINSKY in capital letters.

I asked if she was going to knock and she said, "I just want to see."

The downstairs window had a net curtain to stop folk like us from looking in. On the sill in front of the curtain, a skinny geranium strained towards the light, its single orange flower pressed against the windowpane.

Olive said, "We shouldn't be here." She started to shiver but still she didn't move. She stood looking at the name on the door until a clap of thunder cracked the sky open and the rain came crashing down. We pulled up our hoods and ran.

17

1973

The constable ducks his head as he comes in behind the sergeant and straight away the living room and everything in it shrinks. I still don't know his name and I decide to think of him as Gulliver. Dad sits next to me on the miniature settee and the sergeant takes the tiny armchair. Gulliver lifts the piano stool with one giant hand and plonks it down beside him. Mum has taken to her bed, one less of them for me to worry about.

The sergeant asks if I saw Olive the morning she disappeared.

I shake my head. This is my first, silent lie.

Gulliver looks down and scribbles something in his notebook. The sergeant keeps his eyes on me and I have to stop myself from looking away. "You're sure?" he says.

I nod this time. Another silent lie. But, even if I wanted, I couldn't tell him much. I only saw Olive for a couple of seconds that morning.

"It's just you must have left the house about the same time – to get the bus?"

I tell him, "I'm always late."

Above us, a bedroom floorboard creaks and Gulliver's eyes flick to the ceiling then back to me. "You were up early enough the other morning," he says, "at the window." This is the first time I've heard his voice. It's big and rumbly just like him. The sergeant shoots him a sharp look and he goes back to taking notes.

"So you were late," the sergeant says. "You didn't miss the bus though?"

"No, I just made it."

He looks hard at me. "She couldn't have left that long before you. You might've seen her up ahead on Springfield Road."

I shrug. "Maybe she went the other way."

There are two ways out of the square, the road that leads on to William Street, and the back lane past the Doigs' rabbit hutch on to Springfield Road. But there's no maybe about it. I made sure I went the other way. The sun was sharp that morning, and we came out at the same moment. Olive slammed the yellow door behind her and the bang rang around the square. She squinted across at me, and her hand went up as if she was about to wave, but I didn't stop to see.

I swivelled and stepped back inside like I'd forgotten something. I'd managed to avoid her for the last four years and that's the way I wanted it to stay. I didn't know that morning would be my last chance. But now I think about it – maybe she timed it to run into me. Maybe she wanted me to know she really was going. I wouldn't have tried to stop her though, if that's what she was hoping.

Dad lights a cigarette. "Is that it then?"

The sergeant ignores him and smiles at me. "You're doing fine, Grace, nothing to worry about."

I'm not so sure of that. The bedroom floorboards start to creak again and everyone looks up.

Dad says, "My wife's not well." And the sergeant nods sympathetically, but Gulliver doesn't look convinced.

The sergeant turns back to me. "We've been told Olive was in the habit of getting off the bus at Station Road. She rarely went straight home."

As soon as he says "rarely" my heart starts to bump. What else has he been told? How many folk saw me and Olive walking home together the Friday before she vanished? She got off the bus behind me and tapped me on the shoulder. "Get you home?" she said, dead casual, like I shouldn't be surprised, like it was a normal thing for her to ask – and not the first time in four years.

The sergeant says, "Is that right? As a rule, did she get off the bus at Station Road?"

I tell him she did.

"Do you know why?"

I look at him like one of us must be stupid. I've got a good idea, but I'm not telling him. Dad sighs and shifts in his seat, taps his cigarette end in the ashtray. Gulliver looks up from his notebook and makes his eyes go narrow. He's done it once too often and now it seems ridiculous. I have to stop myself from smirking.

The sergeant tries again. "Do you know if she was meeting a boyfriend?"

"I never saw her with a boy." And that is all I have to tell him. There was no boy as far as I know. It's not my fault he hasn't thought to ask about Olive's grandma.

The sergeant gets to his feet. "That's it," he says, "For now."

It's over quicker than I expected but I'm too tense to feel relieved. Plus I don't know what "for now" means but it doesn't sound long enough. Dad stubs out his cigarette and gets up along with the sergeant. They shake hands and move towards the door. Gulliver puts the stool back by the piano and bends to read the title of the sheet music on the stand.

"*Forty Eight Preludes and Fugues by J.S. Bach.*" He turns and looks at me. "Do you play too?"

"Yeah, a bit." But it's nothing to do with him and I can't believe I'm blushing.

"Before and after," he says out of nowhere. "Prelude and fugue, the one leads to the other." He looks hard at me. "You know what fugue means?"

I nod, but I don't say. A flight. Like running away. Dad and the sergeant have disappeared into the hall now and he's still hulking over me. I'm pretty sure he knows there's something I haven't told them. I stay put on the settee and stare down at his big black boots until he goes.

After a moment the front door slams. Dad comes back into the living room and lights another cigarette.

"So you really didn't see her up ahead?"

I say, "I don't remember." This is an outright lie. I remember fine. In the seconds before Olive vanished, I watched through the hall window. I can still picture her, the way the light caught fire in her hair, the ripple in her pleated navy skirt as she swung through the gate and turned to go along the lane. I waited till I couldn't see her any more then I nipped out and went the other way down William Street.

Dad stands with his back to the blank television, sucks in smoke and lets it drift out through his nostrils, all the while watching me. But there's nothing he can say that would make me feel guilty right now. He's the one in the wrong. In my head, I start to count out the pills again. One Valium, two Valium, three Valium, four... I'm mad at him. I hope he knows. I hope he sees it in my eyes. Five Valium, six Valium... But it's none of my business, according to him. I shouldn't have been poking about.

Finally, he says, "Fair enough."

I can't make up my mind if he's talking about Olive or the pills.

18

1969

Once we'd started we couldn't stay away. We took the shortcut through the alley every day, sneaking past the narrow cottage and the black door. The sun never seemed to reach it, not on the way to school in the morning, not on the way home. When we got near, we'd stop talking and speed up, ducking and darting past the window. The geranium soon dropped its petals and they lay shrivelling on the sill. We didn't even think of knocking. Some doors seemed more shut than others and the Dolinskys' didn't look like the kind that welcomed unexpected callers. We shivered in the shadows and held our breath till we were back out in the light.

On the railway bridge and on the bridge over the river, we sang "Ob-La-Di Ob-La-Da", our favourite song that year, about Desmond and Molly Jones. How he works in the market and she sings with the band and their lives go on. Right up until the final verse – then they swap places and it's Molly's turn to work in the market now. And the bit we liked the best – Desmond puts on Molly's make-up and starts singing with the band. We decided we didn't blame him. Who would want to be the man, shouting *RIPE BANANAS, SWEET TOMATOES* all day long? We weren't so sure what was in it for Molly though. Olive said maybe she got fed up singing the same old love songs every night. Maybe she felt like shouting her head off for a change.

One afternoon on the way home from school, we got to wondering what it would be like if we swapped places with each other. I reckoned the best bit would be having all of Olive's spotless socks. The ankle socks with candy hoop cuffs. The knee-highs with forget-me-nots embroidered down the sides. Socks that never lost their partners. Olive decided if she could be me, the best bit would be having a mum with a job to go to. She'd rather put up with odd socks than the non-stop nagging she got at home. *Do you call this shambles tidy? Pick this up. Put that away.* According to Olive, what bugged her mum the most was that she had a family of living, breathing, dirty human beings who ate and peed and farted and sweated. She'd rather have a bunch of robots. The beds would never be unmade. Robots didn't need to sleep. They didn't need feeding either. So no crumbs or washing up.

We stopped on the road bridge and looked down at a heron knee-deep in the river, grey as boulders, still as stone – and Olive said she wished her dad was around more. It felt safer when he was at home. Her mum had been on a diet ever since she had the baby and the slimming pills she got from the doctor made her rush about like crazy, plus she was permanently snappy. She only sat down to give Bobby his bottle and the whole house reeked of Domestos.

I chanted the Domestos jingle, "Domestos kills ninety-nine point nine nine per cent of all known germs. DEAD."

And Olive said, "Yeah, but they don't count. It's the ones that survive that drive her crazy. She can't see them to get at them. They could be anywhere. They could be everywhere. She cleans and kills all day long."

The heron craned its neck, dipped its head into a gleaming black eddy, came up with nothing as far as we could see.

"I bet a heron never went on a diet," Olive said. "And you know what happened to my birthday cake?"

I nodded. She told me already. Her mum threw the leftover cake in the bin. She didn't want temptation in the house, and there was nothing but Ryvita in their biscuit tin. I thought about my mum and how she squeezed herself into her extra-firm corselet, that secret layer of armour that held her in and smoothed her out. She was nothing like Olive's mum and there were always chocolate biscuits in our tin. I asked if the cardigan was still in the sideboard drawer, and Olive said it was last time she checked and she was pretty sure the ragman hadn't been round yet.

"It suited you," I said.

"D'you think so?"

"Uh-huh. It made you pretty."

She blushed and looked away. She wasn't used to compliments from me. The heron unfolded its wings and flapped off downstream to stand knee-deep in a new spot, and we turned and tiptoed into the alley. We didn't say another word till we were through and safe on the railway bridge. We waved to the signalman and he shook his head. There wouldn't be an InterCity any time soon but we didn't care and we sang "Ob-La-Di Ob-La-Da" all the way home to the square.

19

1973

That Friday before Olive went missing, she got off the bus behind me and tugged my sleeve. "Get you home," she said, and we fell into step like four years hadn't passed, like Peter hadn't died and we were still innocent.

Walking side by side we didn't need to meet each other's eyes. I let her do the talking and studied our feet. She had on the cream patent shoes, slick as mirrors, with little heels that clip-clopped as she went along. My shoes were black and flat and soundless. She said it would be her sixteenth birthday soon and she still had the troll I gave her. It was about all she had left from those days. You grow out of your toys, your books, your clothes. The troll went everywhere with her though. She pulled it out of her school bag to show me. It was smaller than I remembered but its face was still happy and fierce under the shock of electric blue hair. She told me she sometimes combed it for luck, or if she had a question. Like what should she do next? She needed all the help she could get these days to make up her mind. She would be leaving school soon.

She said, "Have you thought about what you'll do when you leave?"

I shrugged. "University maybe." I reckoned this sounded better than admitting I didn't want to leave at all. I wasn't ready even to start thinking about it yet.

She said, "I wish I had that kind of ambition. What subject d'you want to study?"

I had no idea, except it wouldn't be science or maths, or anything to do with numbers. She wasn't so impressed with that.

"I'll be old enough to leave next week," she said. "Officially. You'll be in the same boat soon. You should start preparing."

She stepped off the kerb ahead of me and clip-clopped across the road. We used to clip-clop round the square in our mothers' old high heels thinking we sounded all grown-up. She probably thought she was grown-up for real now, but she didn't seem much different to me. I called out after her, "Just because you can leave doesn't mean you should."

She looked back at me. "I have some work experience at least." Meaning I didn't, I suppose.

She'd been the Saturday girl at Lizzie's almost a year now. She told me she only got to sweep up the hair clippings at first and make the teas and coffees, but these days she got to do the shampoos as well. "The tips are a lot better," she said. "But it feels weird touching folk I hardly know." Her eyes were full of doubts and dread.

It was my turn to say something next but I wasn't sure what. We walked on up the hill for a bit while I thought about it. Normally, she got off the bus two stops before me in Station Road, not far from the alley where her grandma lives. Is that where she went? Not that I cared if she did or she didn't. I only asked to break the silence. "D'you still go to see your grandma?"

She stopped in her tracks and gave me a hurt look. "I don't have anybody else. My grandma's all I've got."

I knew anybody else probably meant me but I said, "What about Morag?"

She said, "Morag's okay but there's stuff I can't tell her."

A pair of first-year girls trudged past us, lugging hockey sticks and school bags. I couldn't have told you who they were, but Olive said hello and their names as well, and they grinned back at her. One of them flicked a wary sideways glance at me. Maybe I seemed unfriendly. I didn't mean to be. It's just I wasn't interested in random folk who had nothing to do with me. I didn't need to know their names the way Olive did, didn't need them to like me.

I started to move on again and she said, "Wait up." She pointed down at her shoes. "I can't go home in these."

She sat down on a garden wall and handed me the troll while she undid the buckles on her school bag and dug out a pair of flat, black lace-ups. The troll's body was still warm from her hands. I didn't want to touch it, didn't want to feel that close to her, plus I didn't know why she had to give it to me anyway when she could just as easily have laid it down beside her on the wall. I held it dangling by its hair and hovered over her while she shucked off the cream patent shoes, put on the black ones and tied the laces.

Her nails were bitten down to the quick, raggedy and raw, and when she looked up her eyes were fierce. "I'll be leaving next week," she said, "On my birthday."

"So what'll you do then? Work full-time at Lizzie's?"

She looked baffled for a second. "No, I mean really leaving. Not just school. Leaving home. Leaving this whole town forever."

I held the troll out to her but she ignored it.

"Aren't you going to ask me why?"

I didn't need to ask though. I already knew. I watched her bury the patent shoes at the bottom of her school bag. Maybe she was hoping I would try to talk her out of going. Maybe she wanted me to tell her I didn't blame her any more. But I didn't blame her in the first place. More like she blamed herself. It's just some things can't be forgotten. Some things are never over. In any case, I didn't believe she would really leave. I thought it was just talk. And what was the point of talking about something that wouldn't happen, something we both just wished?

20

1969

Of course, I could've told her Vanessa Reid would pick some other girl to sit with on the high-school bus. Olive never stood a chance, I knew that all along. The chosen one was Patsy Pringle. Olive found out in the cloakroom before the morning bell. Patsy had been waiting for her, especially to rub it in. That afternoon on the way home from school, I had to act like I was sorry. And I kind of was but I was glad as well. Vanessa wasn't going to be Olive's new best friend, and we could carry on the same as usual, at least until she went to high school and that was months away. I started singing "Ob-La-Di" to try and cheer her up, but she was in a mood and she wouldn't join in. She said singing in the street was childish. She said I had no feelings. And Vanessa could at least have told her to her face instead of leaving it to Patsy. Plus Patsy didn't have to smirk. Of course, she was an incomer, same as Vanessa. That lot stuck together.

I pointed out we stuck together too. But Olive said that was different. We didn't have much choice. At the bottom of the alley, she hissed at me to shush and tiptoed on ahead. She did this every time and I kept trying to tell her it was daft. Tiptoes only made us look like we were up to something, but she would never listen.

I hung back now and watched her sneak deeper and deeper into the alley. A bit down from her grandma's, she turned to see where I'd got to and waited till I moved. Then she tiptoed on again, taking tiny careful steps till she was at the door. Usually, she sped up before she got that far but not this time. She didn't duck or dart. She didn't tiptoe by. She stood there staring at the door – and I just knew what she was thinking.

I broke into a gallop. But her hand was on the knocker

already. She lifted it and let it go, and the clatter ricocheted up and down the alley, ripping through the quiet shadows. After a second, the net curtain at the downstairs window twitched and her grandma peered out. Olive waved and said, "Hello Grandma, we found out where you live." Her grandma couldn't hear and she just shook her head and let the curtain fall. We didn't get a smile.

We turned and looked at each other while we waited to see if she came to the door. We weren't sure she would. We didn't say a word, just kept our eyes locked tight and listened to the wind chimes at the top end of the alley, and listened to the cars growling past the bottom end, the river rushing through the town and, after a while, beneath those familiar sounds, we began to hear something else – quick and constant – seeping out through the seams of the black door.

Finally, it opened and the sound swelled and flooded out. Olive's grandma stepped into the alley and we saw all the clocks in the lobby behind her. Not just one or two clocks. Everywhere we looked, a different kind of clock looked back at us, all ticking out together. It was ten to four by the grandfather clock at the foot of the stairs, ten to four by the wall clock at the far end of the lobby, ten to four by the clutter of little clocks on the shelf above the coat rail.

Olive said, "So how are you today, Grandma?"

And her grandma smiled and said, "All the better for seeing you." When she smiled, you could tell her teeth were false. They were too big and white and even. She had on a navy apron with big white polka dots and deep pockets, and purple velvet slippers worn thin at the toes. She kissed Olive on the forehead. An Ordinary Kiss but not automatic, you could tell she meant it.

"This is a lovely surprise," she said. "But you know you're not supposed to come here behind your mother's back.

Olive hung her head and tried to look like she was sorry. She wasn't though. She couldn't wait to say something else. "Did you hear the astronauts are on their way back now?"

We all gazed up at the narrow strip of sky above the alley. Somewhere up there, Apollo 10 was getting ready to re-enter the earth's atmosphere.

"They saw the Dark Side," Olive said.

Her grandma shuddered and quickly crossed herself. She said nobody could go to the Dark Side and come back the same. She didn't like to think about how cold it must be up there and she was worried for the astronauts' immortal souls.

I looked at Olive and she shrugged back. I wanted to ask her grandma why she had so many clocks when there could only be one time, and if she was a Catholic because Olive wasn't one. But, before I got the chance, we heard a scratchy, old man's voice from deep inside the house calling out – *who's there?*

Olive's grandma froze for a second then pressed a finger to her lips and whispered, "You'd better go." She fished a shilling out of her apron pocket and handed it to Olive. "Share it with your friend, mind." I didn't get a name. Maybe she couldn't remember. She didn't stop to hear us say thanks but just before she closed the door she whispered, "Come again."

She wasn't supposed to encourage us. Even I knew that. If she'd said don't come back, we would not have dared. What happened next wouldn't only be our fault.

21

1973

The police have barely left the square when June comes looking for me. "I won't come in," she says, as if I'd asked. Her voice is quick and breathy... something about chaos... and Saturday morning... but I'm distracted by her lipsticky mouth, the way she shapes the glistening scarlet words and how they clash with her too tight, pink mohair sweater. Her breasts jut out like a ledge and remind me of my old Sindy doll, the one with bendy arms and legs.

"So anyway," she says. "I mentioned you." She leans in closer and I smell her perfume, something flowery with a hint of vanilla. She says, "Lizzie's willing to give you a try."

Finally, it penetrates – she's offering me a job. Me. I stare at her now like I'm stupid and she rushes on. "You'll be kept busy, mind. But it's not hard. You'll be fine."

She's serious. I don't know what to say. I haven't been near a hairdresser since she gave me that pixie cut. The living room door swings open and Dad breezes through the hall. She gazes past me and starts to smile, but he's oblivious for once. He strides upstairs two at a time and, for a second, her smile dies. The spell of lipstick and powder is broken and I catch a glimpse of the bare, lonely face below.

"So are you interested?" Her smile slips back in place. "It's just we need someone to start next Saturday."

Straight off, I think – no. Saturday's too soon. I need time to get used to the idea of a job, any kind of job. And how would I fit in at the salon? I look all wrong – shaggy hair and raggy nails. Plus I'm no good with people, not chatty like Olive. They must be desperate to even consider me. Besides, I can't say yes just like that. It's Olive's job we're talking about.

I say, "She might be back by next Saturday."

June turns and nods towards the Broadfoots' house. "I don't think so. Would *you* run back home to a mother like that?"

I wonder what she thinks she knows and how much of it's just guessing.

"Anyway," she says, "Lizzie doesn't want her back. In fact, we were hoping she might leave and save us letting her go. She was too forward with the clients. You know what she's like – always too intense. Remember that business with the towels? Practically stalking me."

I give her a blank look. There's no way I'm telling her I remember. It's painful now to think about all those times Olive went knocking on her door and how I wished she'd stop. I was her best friend back then, supposedly, but I always knew that really I was only the best she could do. It was like she was stranded on the far side of the moon, cut off from the warm world where she believed people like June and Vanessa lived, special people who had the power to make her feel special too just by being near and breathing the same air.

June shakes her head. "A funny girl."

I gaze at her gooey lips. They're far too much. Someone should tell her, but I just say, "She only wanted to help."

June raises her plucked-thin eyebrows. "Maybe."

I wish she would go now but she presses on. "You get the best tips on Saturday and Lizzie says, if you want it, the job's yours. If not, we can always get somebody else."

I think about the money. It's tempting. But I like the long lie-ins on Saturday mornings, like them better than Sundays. There's no rush on Saturdays, no Monday looming. I know what Mum will say if I turn down this chance though: I mooch too much, get too much pocket money, don't appreciate it, that sort of thing. She left school at my age. She's always telling me – she paid digs, stood on her own two feet. And okay a Saturday job at Lizzie's isn't two feet, not even one, but it's a toe at least and I wouldn't need the pocket money, wouldn't need to appreciate so much.

I gaze at June's skinny eyebrows and sigh. I have to say yes but I can't bring myself to thank her.

She says, "Are you sure?"

And I nod, though really I'm only sure about the money. I'm not sure about the job at all.

"Good," she says, "then it's a deal. Eight-thirty on Saturday, okay?"

I say, "Uh-huh," and she gives me a doubtful look. Another funny girl, I bet that's what she's thinking. I bet she's already regretting putting in a word for me.

She steps back as if to go – hesitates. "I saw the police were here," she says. "They were round at Lizzie's earlier, asking did we notice anything different about Olive lately and did she have a boyfriend? I told them I'd be very surprised." She stops and wrinkles up her nose. "Like I said – a funny girl. Always came across too desperate. Boys don't want that."

She turns and totters down the path in her flimsy sandals and that too tight mohair sweater. The evening is too warm for mohair and she has a cheek calling Olive desperate.

As soon as I close the door, Mum and Dad appear at the top of the stairs. It looks like they've been waiting for her to leave and they bustle downstairs now into the kitchen and he boils the kettle and makes himself a coffee while she digs the frying pan out of the cupboard. She says, "It'll be about fifteen minutes," and he wanders through to the piano, doesn't even look at me.

Sometimes, it's hard to keep hold of what's true. Maybe the Benylin bottle was left over from some old cough. Maybe I didn't count out her tablets... one Valium, two Valium... Maybe they weren't twenty-four short and I'm the crazy one here.

He starts to play the tune for the Nimble bread ad, "I Can't Let Maggie Go". He hasn't been home this early in weeks and I can't remember when he last sat down to play. I realise now I've been missing it. I even miss his foot thudding. Mum flits about the kitchen in her stocking soles. Of course, the Nimble tune is meant to be a message for her. He's hoping she'll melt. But is she listening? Does she even care that he can't let Maggie go? And anyway, her name is Marion.

She scrapes the burnt stew into the bin and I sit at the kitchen table and pretend to do the homework I didn't get in class today. I'll have to write a sick note and forge her signature before I go back to school. I've decided on gastroenteritis because it's more seasonal. There aren't a lot of head colds around at this time of year.

Mum fills the scorched pan with hot soapy water now and leaves it to soak in the sink. She makes French toast and a pot of tea and asks me to go and tell Dad it's ready though she is nearer the door. I gather up my books and his evening paper. He reads it on the train and drops it on the kitchen table when he gets in and never looks at it again. I used to read the comic strips, but not so much since I discovered the small ads: lonely hearts, property to let, situations vacant. Love, shelter, money, everything you need to get by. I hope Olive knows about the small ads. She's going to need them. I tell Dad the food's out and take the paper up to my room for later, dump it on the bed along with my books. The piano is silent now. His foot stops thudding and the heart goes out of the house.

Back in the kitchen, the three of us sit round the table and they don't look at each other. They take it in turns to ask questions about my day.

Did I get the result of the trig test?

"Not yet." This is true. But only because I wasn't there to get it.

What did I have for school dinner?

"Hot pot."

Didn't I have hot pot just the other day?

"I don't remember." The whole truth is I can't remember the last time I ate school dinner. They don't know I go to the café.

And the pudding?

"Tapioca." I make a face. "I didn't eat it." The second part at least is true.

So what did June want?

Finally a question where I don't have to make up the answer. "I've got a Saturday job – at Lizzie's." It still doesn't feel real to me and I'm surprised how quick they are to believe it. They seem pleased, proud in fact of my new career making coffee and sweeping up hair.

Dad wants to know how much it pays.

"I forgot to ask."

Mum says probably not much but the tips should be good on a Saturday. She hasn't touched her French toast yet and he looks at her plate now and says, "You should eat something," the first words he's said directly to her since we all sat down.

She shoots him a killer and starts to tear her French toast to pieces.

He says her name, soft and pleading.

And she sets her lips in a thin tight line and goes on tearing.

He tries again. "Marion, please."

She ignores him and turns to me. "You're not the only one with a new job. Did you know that?" Her voice skids up and up. "Did you know your dad had another job? Not just a job, a whole new other life?"

I stare at her twisting lips and the raw rage in her eyes. The trouble with anger is it makes you want to slap its ugly face.

She turns to him and says, "Why don't you explain to Grace? Tell your daughter where you were last night. And all those other nights."

But I don't want to know. I scrape back my chair and get up from the table. And Dad just sits there looking sorry as I walk out of the room.

22

1969

Most mornings, I came round to the screech of the cold water pipe when Mum filled the kettle. Then she put on the radio and the muffled chant of the weather forecast would drift up through my bedroom floor. But now and then there would be a morning when I woke up to silence and straight away I knew somebody was dead. It made her late if she lost a patient near the end of a shift. She couldn't just go home and leave the body for the day staff. She had to close their eyes, take off rings, straighten fingers and pack the orifices, all the body's holes, so what was inside – the pee and snot and shit and stuff – wouldn't leak out and smell. And after all that, she still had the report to give before she could get away.

Those mornings, there would be an empty feeling down in the kitchen while Dad and I ate breakfast. Our spoons clattered against our cereal bowls and echoed round the room and we could never think of anything to say.

*

After Apollo 10 splashed down in the Pacific Ocean, all our lives went back to their old earthbound state. In the playground, the boys gave up chanting the countdown. In our classrooms, the atmosphere was flat and afternoons went on and on. Olive and I couldn't wait to get out. We raced through the school gates, straight down the high street and over the river into the alley to knock on the black door. Olive's grandma would come out and stand on the step, pulling the door behind her so we couldn't see in. We could still hear the clocks but we didn't hear the old man's voice again.

She always had on the same purple slippers and the same

blue-and-white polka dot pinny. Sometimes she produced a couple of buttered treacle scones from the pinny pocket, sometimes just custard creams which we saved for later. The scones were home-baked and still warm, and we ate them dripping butter where we stood while Olive's grandma asked us things like how was school today, and were we warm enough? Did we not have pullovers? It might be almost summer for the rest of the town but not where she lived and she could see us shivering. She never asked what happened to the oyster-pink cardigan and Olive never had to tell her it was in the sideboard drawer waiting for the ragman. Maybe her grandma guessed it was better not to know. She always asked how Bobby was doing. Was he sleeping through the night yet? Could he sit up on his own? She asked after Peter as well but she never said his name. It was always *that brother of yours*. I didn't think it was fair that Bobby got his name when he was hardly even a proper person yet and Peter was eleven, the same age as me. Plus I got the feeling, if I wasn't there, she'd call me *that friend of yours*. That's all I was to her of course – Olive's friend. I don't suppose she wanted to see me every day and I'm not sure why I wanted to see her. I only know I did, more and more.

One time, she told us that her own first name was Bella and it meant beautiful in Italian. She winked at us and said, "Not that I was ever what you'd call beautiful."

Olive said, "You are to me."

And her grandma shook her head and laughed. "I'm not Italian either."

I wanted Olive to ask how many clocks she had altogether and Olive kept forgetting. The clocks didn't seem to matter to her but they mattered to me. The time was always on my mind when we were at her grandma's door. I'd listen to the seconds ticking by, shuffling from foot to foot, desperate to get going before something went wrong. This town was too wee and too nosy for us to keep our visits secret long. Folk often passed while we were there and, sooner or later, somebody was sure to tell Olive's mum they'd seen us. They wouldn't even know they were telling tales and Olive wasn't meant to be there. She'd be in big trouble then.

If Olive's grandma only gave us custard creams, we put them in our pockets and the visit would be over quick. If we got scones, we stayed as long as it took Olive to finish hers, and this could be ages if she did too much of the talking and didn't listen enough. When her scone was finally done, she'd thank her grandma for it and say, "We'll see you soon." And her grandma would cross herself and say, "If the good Lord spares me." I thought it was a funny thing to say, as if she didn't want us to be sure of seeing her again.

One time after we said goodbye, I asked Olive if her grandma was a Catholic. Did she go to St Joseph's?

And Olive turned and said, "So what if she does?"

"It's just your mum and dad go to the ordinary church."

She said, "So?" Like she didn't care. But her face went red.

And that's when I spotted Peter, over her shoulder, shooting out of Station Road on to the railway bridge, running hard like he was being chased. I decided not to mention it. Right then, I didn't think her brother was the subject to put her in a better mood. By the time we got on to the railway bridge, there was no sign of Peter. I thought maybe he hadn't seen us, but even if he had – so what? I didn't think it would matter that much. I clung on to the parapet while Olive waved to the signalman. He looked up and shook his head and we both groaned, even though we knew there was no InterCity at that time of day.

We walked on and Olive said, "What if the Lord doesn't spare her? What if that's the last time I see her?" He couldn't spare her grandma forever, she said, and she looked worried all the way home.

23

1973

The Evening Times is light on news and heavy on football and advertising. I sit cross-legged on my bed with the paper spread open at the horoscopes. Since Olive went missing, I've started checking both our forecasts. The day for which they're cast is almost over by the time I read them and tonight I take some weird kind of comfort out of seeing that they're wrong again. Olive's scope has no idea she's even missing, never mind where she might be, and mine gives no hint I should get back to school tomorrow. Olive is Taurus, a stubborn bull, and I am Pisces, a slippery fish, and our signs pretty much sum us up. Mum would agree with the slippery bit for sure. She'd love to know what I'm thinking and I can't imagine anything worse. She's getting ready for work now, padding back and forth between the bathroom and the bedroom, and I tense up each time she passes my door.

The sky through the window is rosy, an omen of fine weather for my hike up to Pisgah Wood tomorrow. I'll take something to drink this time, make sandwiches before I set off, have a proper picnic in some dappled, mossy clearing – no stolen milk and no dead lamb. I flick to the small ads and rooms to let. The cheaper the room the harder the ad is to decipher, almost no proper words, just abbreviations: S/rm, Cecil St, £6pw, wk in adv, no students, DHSS. Today this is the only one I reckon Olive can afford. I turn to situations vacant and search for suitable jobs. Trainee hairdressers are the worst paid, shop assistants not much better unless you have experience, which she doesn't. Half her pay will go on rent. I never thought about stuff like this before she left. It's kind of scary and my heart is bumping. A floorboard creaks outside my door and I look up and see the handle turning. Mum. I wish she would knock. I slide the evening paper under my pillow before she walks in and my cheeks go hot, as if an interest in the small ads is proof I'm all kinds of devious.

Her nurse's tunic is blindingly white, almost a blank, and her head seems to float in mid-air on its own. She comes over to the foot of my bed and hovers there until I say, "Is that you off then?"

"In a minute." She sits down beside me, and her voice is flat. "He lost his job. Gordon Brothers went out of business weeks ago."

I say *oh*, just as flat, and hope that's it.

She works her lips from side to side and I look away. I don't want to hear any more.

"He's been lying to us all this time. He lied to me. Lied to you." Her voice sharpens. "Unless you knew, did you know? Did you know he joined a band?"

I tell her no, and it's the truth. I guessed he had a secret – yes. But not a band, never that.

She says, "Look at me."

I turn and gaze at the fob watch pinned to her tunic. The time is upside down. I watch the second hand tick down to twelve and start back up again, while bubbles of relief rise in my throat now. A band is not so bad and maybe the woman with the blue guitar case is nothing to worry about after all, just the guitarist.

Mum says, "So what did you think he was doing all those nights he didn't come home?"

I shake my head and choke back a gurgle. "Overtime, I suppose."

"Till after midnight? You never let on he was staying out so late. Why d'you cover up for him?"

I don't know how to explain – except it felt easier, that's all, just like it's easier to say nothing now. There's no point trying to tell her he didn't lie, not to me anyway. He didn't say a thing. I pluck a tuft out of the candlewick bedspread and roll it between my thumb and forefinger. "What kind of band? Is it jazz?" I want it to be jazz.

She sniffs the air. "Has he been smoking in your room again?"

I tell her he smokes everywhere. This is true, and it's lucky there's no difference between the smell of his smoke and mine.

She sniffs again. "They've got a residency in some hotel, Tuesday and Thursday nights, Saturday lunchtime as well. It's not a living. Split five ways the money's nothing." She checks her fob watch and gets to her feet. "You won't find it so funny when the redundancy money runs out."

She still hasn't said if it's jazz. She stalks out of the room, slams the door behind her, and I flop back on the bed. The newspaper rustles beneath my pillow. I can't remember why I hid it now. But we all hide stuff.

*

She's in a slamming mood tonight and when she leaves for work the front door crashes shut behind her and the whole house shakes. She takes the tension with her, takes it to ward 7 at the hospital where she can nurse it all night long. Dad goes back to the piano, starts to play a slow, meandering tune I've never heard before. So slow I can't remember what came before or guess what's coming next and I keep getting lost in the present riff. I wonder *when* he learned it, and *where*, and *who* with. And what does she sound like, the woman with the blue guitar case? I want to tell him he sounds fine without her. I hope he knows he doesn't need her. I wish Mum could hear him the way I do now, when he is deep inside the music. Maybe then she'd understand she can't stop him dreaming.

The phone rings in the hall and I spring up from the bed and fly downstairs to get it so he can go on playing. I don't want to break his mood and I keep my voice down when I pick up the receiver.

Claire cuts across my hello. "So are you really ill or just bunking off?" She never says her name or hello back, just launches straight into whatever's on her mind and leaves me to catch up.

I start to mutter something about gastroenteritis and she butts in, "Why are you whispering?"

"I'm not."

"You are," she says flatly. "So will I see you on the bus tomorrow?"

I tell her I'm not sure if I'll be better by the morning.

She clicks her tongue as if to say she knows I'm fibbing. In any case, she isn't calling out of concern for my health. "Guess what?" she says. "Morag's seen her."

"Seen who?" I don't feel like guessing.

"Who d'you think? Olive, last night, across the road from Morag's house, just standing there in the dark." Claire's the one whispering now but I don't point this out. She says, "There wasn't enough light to make out if the hair was red but Morag swears she'd know Olive's outline anywhere, what with her being so lanky. She went out to try and talk to her and she heard footsteps running off."

Claire pauses for a second. "Are you still there?"

"Uh-huh."

"D'you think it really was her?"

"You know Morag's weird. It could've been anyone."

"Yeah, but why would she make up something like that?"

I have no idea. I peer through the hall window and across the square to the Broadfoots' house. No clue there. I can't believe Olive would show herself to Morag Ross and not me.

"Did she tell anybody else?"

"I don't think so – no."

I start to wonder why Morag picked on Claire. "Did she just come up to you and tell you all this stuff or what? I mean why you?"

"I don't know," Claire says sarcastically. "Maybe because I was there. She asked where you were, why you weren't on the bus."

"Well, I think she's seeing things and I'm telling you she's weird." Next door, Dad shifts into another number and my stomach lurches. "I have to go now. I feel sick."

112

"Are you really ill then?"

I pretend I don't hear. I'm getting tired of all my lies. I put down the phone and tell myself again – Morag must be seeing things. Seeing what she wants to see. It's easy in the dark. Easy if you're missing someone.

24

1969

The new neighbour made an effort with the front garden, kept the grass down and trimmed the hedges. The back garden was a different story though. She only went out there for two reasons, wading through the long grass in her high-heeled pink mules to hang out the towels, or if she spotted Dad. He grew potatoes, beetroot and cabbages, and I helped him with the hoeing. The week Apollo 10 returned to earth, she came over to the fence and told us that her favourite tune was "Stranger on the Shore" and did we know the crew had it on tape? Could we imagine how Acker Bilk's clarinet would sound up there in space?

"Out of this world," Dad said and they both smiled. She asked if he could teach her how to play it on the piano, and he agreed to give her a lesson.

Mum wasn't happy when she heard. She said June's taste was predictable and did the silly woman really think she could learn to play – just like that? One lesson wouldn't be much use. Did she not understand you needed to practise, and how could she practise without a piano? Maybe she was hoping one lesson would lead to another. He better make it clear he didn't have the time.

He said, "Fine."

But it wasn't fine with Mum. It was anything but and when he tried to kiss her she pushed him away and said, "Tell her no."

He sighed and gave her one of his long looks. He looked at me that way sometimes, like he was disappointed and trying hard to understand, and it always made me sorry. But she just said, "You heard me."

"You're tired," he said, "I wish you'd give up working nights. We don't need the extra money any more."

She said, "Extra?"

"Okay, not extra. This is not about the money. This is about *us*."

"You think you can just change the subject?" Mum said. "This is about *her*. You tell her no. Okay?" She slammed out of the kitchen so hard the walls bounced and the dishes on the draining board rattled.

I must have been frowning because he turned and rubbed the spot between my eyebrows with his index finger. He said, "Don't look so worried."

I suppose he thought their row upset me, and maybe it should have. But right at that moment I was only thinking that I didn't want Mum quitting the night shift, didn't want our routine changing. I knew the nights must be lonely for him with only the piano and a kid for company – and I was kind of sorry for him. But it was better just the two of us, and not only for me. On her nights off, he hardly touched the piano – the thing he loved the most next to her. It must've been hard for him to keep away. They sat and watched the telly instead. I missed the music, missed the rhythm of his foot thudding. And his secret audience, I missed them too. Mum had no idea about them. He never let her hear him dreaming.

*

We didn't think much of it the first time. It was just another weekday night. Olive went to collect the laundry basket and June didn't answer the door. Olive was disappointed but I didn't care and we played hopscotch instead.

The next night and the next, I watched from my back garden while Olive knocked and waited, knocked again then turned away, biting her lip. We were sure June was at home because her two-tone grey Anglia was parked outside and she never left the square without it. She couldn't walk far in her high heels and she never wore flats. The car hadn't moved as far as we could tell. We hadn't seen her leave for work. We hadn't seen her coming home. We hadn't seen the usual weary women who came in the evening to get their hair done cheap. We knew she must be in there though. We saw her lights go on at night.

I'm not sure why I didn't tell Olive about the last time I'd seen June. I just didn't. June had answered the door to Dad the day after he fell out with Mum. I'd watched him and June from our back garden while Mum stood and waited at the kitchen door and the whole time Mum had looked straight through me like I wasn't there.

Three days in a row, the same peach towels hung out on the line. We could tell they were the same because a bird shat on the towel at the far end of the row, and the bird shit dried and flaked and faded till all that was left was the ghost of a stain. Olive was sure something was up. She seemed to think we should care. I didn't see why we should. I reckoned it was up to June if she answered the door or not – but try telling that to Olive. She just said, "What if she's ill?"

I don't remember why I let her talk me into going to the door with her. I know I didn't want to. I wished she'd take the hint but she still had the idea that June was her friend. This time, she decided we should go to the front door instead of the back. She didn't say why, but I knew she was hoping June wouldn't guess it was her again. June's door faced north, the same as mine, and it was cold on both our doorsteps. But my door was red. The blue door made it feel colder somehow. Olive knocked on the door, too loud, and I cringed and looked away. On the other side of the square, the sun was shining on the Broadfoots' yellow door. Bobby's pram was parked on the garden path and, for some weird reason, Peter was lurking behind it, gawking over the hood at us.

We didn't get an answer and I tugged at Olive's sleeve and said, "Let's go."

She shook me off and hissed, "What if she's seriously ill?" Her eyes lit up when she said *seriously*, like she was hoping we might have to call 999. "Anyway," she said, "she might be in the bathroom."

She knocked again and I turned and caught Peter ducking behind the pram. I don't know why he bothered. It wasn't like we cared if he saw us or not. I started to tell Olive how daft he looked but she said, "Shh… she's coming."

The blue door edged open and June squinted out at us. For a second, we weren't sure it was her and we both stared. We'd never seen her with her hair down before. It hung loose about her shoulders and hid her ears and blurred the edges of her face. Plus she looked so pale and small and not herself in her stocking soles and with no make-up on.

She glared at Olive. "Oh, you again, what do you want now?"

Olive gulped, and it looked sore, like all the words she wanted to say were balled up in her throat.

June clicked her tongue. "Well?"

Olive still couldn't get the words out, and June sighed and glanced past her to me. She sounded more tired than annoyed now. "Tell your dad I understand. I'll find another teacher." She tried to smile but it didn't work so well without lipstick. Her lips were tight and bloodless, and her voice quavered. "Tell him it was nothing personal, just 'Strangers on the Shore'."

I started to nod and she shut the door. For a minute we just stood there, Olive snuffling, me staring at my feet. I didn't want to see her face. I felt bad for her. And the bit that confused me – I felt bad for June as well.

25

1973

Most mornings, I hare down William Street in time to scramble on to the school bus – last one on as usual. But today I'm out the door at five to eight, fifteen minutes early. I need to get going before the kids from the Meadow estate start to make their way down to the bus stop. The fewer folk I have to pass on my way up to Pisgah Wood the better but, mainly, I don't want to run into Claire. She would try to stop me and make me go to school.

I race uphill until the turnoff to the Meadows is safely behind me and the road curves left, flattening out just long enough for me to catch my breath before it starts to climb again. The last time me and Olive were up this way, the town ended around here and the fields began and, shimmering in the distance, there was Pisgah Wood. The sight of it would keep us going.

These days there's no horizon though, just houses stretching on and on, street after street, all much the same and I don't know half their names. The road I'm on is lined on either side with neat bungalows, packed close together but not touching so they still count as detached, and the tips of fast-growing leylandii hedges poke up behind identical garden walls. In another year or two, they'll block out passers-by and they're already managing to make me feel unwelcome.

Two boys in school blazers are trotting down the brae towards me. First years by the looks of them, they make me feel enormous. I wonder why the hurry. Don't they know they're early? They stare at me on their way by and I yank off my school tie, stuff it in my pocket and give them a so-what look. *Yeah, I'm heading in the wrong direction. No, I don't give a damn what you first years think.*

But I do of course. They might tell on me. Though who they'd tell and why they'd bother, I have no idea.

At the top of the hill, I catch a whiff of tar and the bungalows give way to villas. A sea of them – all empty. This is the new Trossachs estate, just recently completed. The builders have cleared off but no one has moved in so far. All the streets are named after the Trossachs mountains you used to be able to see in the distance: Vorlich, Ledi, Lomond and Venue. You can't see the hills for houses now and half the sky is missing. Most folk down in the square don't seem to care that it's all gone. They never came up this far anyway. Olive used to say they didn't think like us. We were wild and stealthy, like foxes, and they were more like mutts. We hid in our den, like foxes. We had no master over us. Our parents didn't count when we were on our own up in Pisgah Wood.

I spot the show home up ahead now and, next to it, a giant placard with a picture of an identical house. It makes the real one seem less real somehow, two-dimensional. A red Cortina is parked in the real drive and, as I creep past, a sharp-faced woman appears at a downstairs window and frowns out at me. Like I shouldn't be walking here. Like she owns the pavement. She has a badge pinned to the lapel of her blue jacket and I guess she must work for the developers and she's probably waiting to show would-be buyers round. I wonder if she's met the Broadfoots yet. I bet she has and she could tell they weren't serious and only there for a nose about. I bet she hates folk like them for wasting her time but she still has to be nice. She wouldn't dare give any adult the dirty look she just gave me. I gaze right through her like I'm not bothered. Whatever she thinks, I'm not a kid. Next year I can leave school. Buy cigarettes and smoke my head off wherever I like and no one can say anything. Get married if I want. Not that I'll want.

I can change my name by deed poll too. I wonder if Olive calls herself May now and if it makes her feel a better person. Brand new. No history. No guilt. If it was that easy I'd change my name as well, never bunk off school again, quit smoking, learn to tell the truth. Not that I lie if I can help it. Not that Dad lied either, come to think of it. Some of us just prefer to keep things to ourselves, that's all. It's only Mum can't tell the difference between a secret and a fib. She doesn't see they're opposites. There'd be no point in secrets if they weren't true.

I plough deeper into the estate past vacant, staring windows, and the smell of tar gets stronger the further in I go. The walls of the new villas are white and glary. They don't have proper gardens yet, just patches of hard baked earth and hard grey concrete paths. Nothing grows. Nothing moves but me. It feels weird, like I'm the only one alive and this place is some kind of ghost.

The newly rolled tarmac road is smooth and glistening. So far it has followed the same route as the old rutted track, but now it changes course and veers off to the left, away from where I want to go, away from Pisgah Wood. Streets branch off on either side of the road: I take the next turn to the right into Vorlich Crescent and what should be the direction of the wood. I get a few steps in before I see it's a cul-de-sac. The tar fumes start to nip my eyes. I try the next turnoff and the next, Ledi Mount, Lomond Rise, and discover one dead end after another, no sign of a through road anywhere. But Pisgah Wood can't be far. I must be almost there.

My eyes are tearing up, and I want to know who decided to cut the wood off from the town and what gives them the right. We were here first, me and Olive. Who bothered to ask us? There used to be a green field here with a herd of red-brown cows. The grass was springy beneath our feet and the cows ambled with us to the edge of the wood and stopped there, wafting clouds of warm sweet breath, waiting to make sure we understood. The field was their place. The wood was ours, and we could hear them lowing as we melted into the shadows.

The silence here today gives me the creeps. The cul-de-sac I'm in looks so much like the last one and the one before it feels like I've been going nowhere, just coming out and going in the same dead end over and over. I reckon Pisgah Wood must be somewhere behind the house at the far end and maybe I can cut through the back. I decide to check it out and I'm starting into the garden when I hear a car, coming fast, whirring over the smooth tarmac.

I dive for cover behind the garden wall and peer over just in time to clock the blue-and-red stripe of a police car zipping by the end of the cul-de-sac. Gulliver is in the passenger seat and my heart starts to pound. What's he doing here? I think the sergeant's driving but I can't see for sure.

I've no idea where the road goes nowadays, or if it goes anywhere. It could be the biggest dead end of all and I'm scared to move in case they come back this way. I stay hunkered down behind the wall for I don't know how long – until it starts to feel stupid and I get cramp in my calves. I'm about to straighten up when I hear the car again, gliding this time. It slows down to a crawl as it gets closer and I sense their eyes scouring the cul-de-sac. Looking for me I suppose. The muscles in my calves are burning and I grit my teeth. That woman in the show home probably called them, told them I was trespassing or something.

It feels like ages before they move off, and my heart's still pounding as I lurch to my feet and hobble up the drive, through the gap between the house and garage and into the back garden. The wood is much closer than I expected. So close I can smell moss and bark, breathe it in. But there's a fence in the way – behind the low concrete wall at the end of the garden, running in both directions as far as I can see, a towering monstrosity with thick steel posts and diamond wire mesh panels. No way forward. No way round. I limp down to the wall and clamber over, stare through the wire mesh at what's left of the field. All the cool damp grass is gone and in its place a strip of churned-up earth and, just yards away, green and shimmering, and so out of reach it might as well be on the moon – Pisgah Wood.

I kick out at the fence and the metal rattles. I can't work out what it's keeping in, or what it's keeping out. Hard-as-nails hedgehogs? Assassin shrews? Pisgah Wood creeping closer while the incomers sleep? I peer through the fence, into dark spaces between the trees, until I remember why I came here in the first place. Remember Olive. Where is she now? Why did I think I might find her here?

Stupid idea. Stupid idea. I kick the fence again and again.

26

1969

Every day now, the frown on Olive's forehead cleared when her grandma answered the door. The Lord had spared her yet again. Hallelujah. You'd think it was a miracle. And every day Olive forgot to ask about the clocks. In the end, I had to.

How many?

And why?

I needed to know.

Olive's grandma said, "I stopped counting after forty. The clocks belong to him, every single one, unless you count the oven timer."

She'd just finished baking and she dusted her floury hands on the polka-dotted apron and, for the first time ever, gave me a proper smile, not just polite stretched lips, but the cosy pleased-to-see-you smile she normally saved for Olive. She said she was glad we came. Some days the sound of all those ticking clocks got on her nerves and she had to fight a powerful urge to fling all the windows open and let the racket out.

From her apron pocket, she took out two warm treacle scones spread with raspberry jam and butter and handed them to us. "He can't abide the front room window open." She pointed at the gutter that ran down the side of the alley. "No garden, you see. Nothing between us and passers-by. He complains they come too close with their footsteps, and their ears, and their eyes."

I wanted to ask why she didn't give him a name, why was he just *he*? And was he worried about running out of time now he was getting old? Were they both? But my mouth was stuffed with scone and jam, and she told us about the winding of the clocks instead. How every evening after dinner he used to take off his wristwatch and turn on the radio to wait for the six o'clock pips. And how Olive's mum and her aunt Sandra never needed to be warned. From when they were big enough to handle their own knives and forks, they knew to sit still and be quiet while he fixed the time, first on his watch, and then went round the house checking every clock, winding and resetting them.

"It could take a while," Olive's grandma said. She glanced back into the house and sighed. "It's too much for him now, of course, since he had his stroke. These days, it's up to me to wind them and he won't rest until it's done."

When she mentioned his stroke, I noticed Olive frowning as if it was the first she'd heard of it, but Olive's grandma didn't stop to explain. She started on another story. "Your mum never got a second's peace growing up in this house. I expect she's told you."

Olive shook her head. "She always says she's too busy to talk about the past."

Her grandma rolled her eyes as if this didn't surprise her. "The clocks and all their ticking never seemed to bother your Aunt Sandra but your mum couldn't block it out. I remember her saying once it made her feel like everything was going too fast and she couldn't keep up. She had to stick her fingers in her ears to get to sleep. She always was the more sensitive one."

This didn't sound much like Olive's mum to me and it was hard to imagine her any age but the age she was now. In my head, she'd always been thirty-five, always keen on killing germs and not exactly sensitive.

"She had guts as well, mind you," Olive's grandma said. "She got her own back on him and his clocks. Did she never tell you?"

Olive shook her head again and her grandma laughed and told us about the night he came home from work to find every clock in every room showing a different time. "Half past one, ten to nine, quarter past three, every time but the right one. Of course, we knew it wouldn't be Sandra. It had to be your mum's doing and she didn't deny it. She wouldn't tell us why though, wouldn't say sorry either. She could be defiant, your mum. It took him hours to put them all back to right."

Olive nodded, and I thought some things never changed. Her mum still didn't say sorry when she should.

Her grandma said, "She must've been about your age then. Looked just like you too."

Olive asked if she had any pictures. I thought it was a funny question. You'd think she would've seen plenty of pictures of her mum as a girl before, but her grandma said, "Wait here. I'll get one."

She stepped back into the hall and drew the door behind her, not quite shut but not open either. We peered into the dark chink between the edge of the door and the jamb but we couldn't see a thing. Any normal grandma would've asked us in. Any normal grandma wouldn't have left us shivering in the alley, and yet her scones were normal, every bit as light and buttery and comforting as my own grandma's. We heard the shuffle of her slippers, the little clocks' tinny ticks, the heavy clunk of a pendulum, the faint whirr of cogs. Out of the corner of my eye, I caught the flicker of someone zipping past the top end of the alley. I didn't think of Peter then, but the speed made me edgy. It was time we got a move on. We'd already been there a lot longer than usual and we'd get in trouble if we were any later home.

I hissed at Olive, "We have to go soon."

And she hissed back, "Just one more minute."

I sighed and started to move away. One minute never ended up being only one. It could end up five or even ten.

She caught my arm and tugged me back. "We can't go right now. That would be rude and anyway it's your fault. You're the one who got her talking about the clocks."

I said, "At least, the clocks are interesting."

"What's that supposed to mean?"

I just looked at her.

Her grandma came back with a snapshot, black and white and dog-eared. Olive snatched it from her and we both stared. The face could almost have been Olive's, the same freckle-smudged nose, the same flare to the nostrils, the same barely there pale brows. But there was something snippier about the mouth, something spikier in the eyes. I wouldn't want to be best friends with a girl like her.

Olive's grandma said, "Keep it if you want."

Olive went on gazing at the photo. She was probably thinking about places she could hide it. And I was thinking – she must be crazy and what if her mum finds it?

She bit her lip and handed it back. "I better not."

Her grandma said, "That's all right."

It wasn't all right though, even I knew that. There was nothing right about any of it.

27

1973

The quiet presses in around me now as Olive's grandma leads me through the hall. The tinny clocks on the shelf have stopped ticking. The wall clock's pendulum doesn't clunk. The grandfather clock is schtum. She tells me she let them all run down, each in their own time, after *he* passed away. *He* must have a name but she still won't say it. She won't even say "my husband" or let him be "Olive's grandpa". I only knocked because her curtains were closed again. I didn't think she would ask me in though. I didn't even want her to answer, not really.

Not at all, I realise now.

The front room is dim. The curtains are a sludgy shade of green and the glow from a small lamp in the far corner only just reaches to where we sit in straight-backed chairs either side of the table. The surface is cluttered with knitting patterns and pins and balls of wool. I look around the room and there are more clocks everywhere. All sorts of clocks. Silent now. Stopped at all sorts of time. She starts to clear the wool into a quilted workbox, and I can hear her breathing, shallow and uneven.

"I've been wondering when you'd come," she says.

I can't think what to say back.

"It's been four years since you came to see me last." She looks across at me and sighs, as if she's been waiting for me all that time, as if I should've known she'd be waiting. Not that I believe she missed me. It's probably just something to say, but it makes me uneasy that she remembers how many years, and I start to wonder how Olive explained it when I stopped coming round with her. What lie did she tell?

Her grandma gives me no clue now, just smiles across at me and says, "You're looking for her, I suppose."

I shrug. I don't want to admit it but I suppose I am.

"You think she might be here? Look in the kitchen. Look upstairs if you like. You might as well. Everyone else has."

She doesn't say who she means by everyone but I can guess at one of them. I picture P.C. Gulliver ducking and squeezing into the cottage, this little room barely able to contain him. I want to go upstairs right now, poke around, see for myself, but that would be too rude. Instead I blurt out, "I took your milk."

She looks blank.

And I say, "Yesterday?"

"Ah."

I wait for her to say something else but that's it, just *ah*. She starts to sort the knitting pins into pairs and push them through loops in the lid of the workbox. The wooden-cased clock on the mantelpiece has stopped at five to twelve and I wonder whether it gave up just before midnight or before midday. I hope it was midnight. Moonless. Pitch dark. The shape of the clock case reminds me of a humpback bridge.

The silence stretches on till finally she says, "I thought maybe Olive took it." She looks up from what she's doing and I watch the hope fading from her eyes. "Oh well," she says like it doesn't matter.

But of course it does. She wanted it to be Olive and it was only me. And now I'm sure she has no idea where Olive is. I thought if anybody knew it would be her. She starts to fold away the knitting patterns and I say, "I didn't drink the milk." I don't know why I feel the need to tell her this. It doesn't make the stealing any better. Worse really. Pointless. But I blunder on, "I don't even like milk unless it's chilled. I mean freezing."

"I'm glad you told me," she says. "Glad you came."

And I don't even know what I'm going to say next until it's out of my mouth. "You should open your curtains. I thought you were dead."

She gazes at me for a moment, half smiling, and says, "Not yet."

128

I can't believe I actually said it. Dead. Just like that.

She nods towards the window. "Open them if you want."

I get up and draw back the curtains as far as they'll go and thin grey light seeps into the room and cancels out the lamp. The room is still dim. The clock on the mantelpiece still says five to twelve. And I think maybe the time doesn't matter to her these days. There can't be much left for her to look forward to with Olive gone. She offers to make me a cup of tea and I tell her I'm sorry I have to get home.

She probably thinks I'm just being polite. But it's true. I am sorry.

*

I race uphill and into the square past a police car parked by June's gate. They've been here a lot lately and I don't think much about it. I'm only a bit late, ten minutes maybe, and I doubt Mum will even notice. She has bigger worries than me right now. In the hall, I stop to catch my breath and I hear her voice through the living room wall, probably on the phone to Marie again. About Dad and how he's let her down, how a secret's as bad as a lie. She doesn't want to know the difference and Marie will go along with her, of course. She always does. Mum likes to complain that Marie has no opinions of her own but it suits her as well some of the time. Marie doesn't contradict her. Not like me.

I pop my head around the living room door to say hello and start to wave before I see she's not on the phone, and she's not alone. She turns and glares at me from her spot on the couch. The sergeant turns in his armchair and Gulliver looms behind him, narrowing his eyes. I try not to blink back. Let him think what he likes. No Dad I notice. He's never around when I need him, and I don't even have to look at Mum again to know she's seething. I can feel her bristling from across the room. I try a small smile on the sergeant in the hope he'll break the silence, and he gives me a long, stony look back.

And now Mum's voice drills through me. "I'm glad you think it's funny. Where have you been all day? And what about yesterday? Don't even think about lying."

Gulliver smirks. "You were seen – this morning."

He doesn't say who by. Maybe one of those boys coming down the hill far too early for the bus. Or maybe that woman at the show house window. More likely her. She thought she owned the pavement. I wouldn't put it past her to call and complain.

"The Trossachs estate," the sergeant says. "What were you doing up there all on your own? Did you meet anybody?"

I tell him no and he says again, "All on your own?"

"Yes on my own." I gaze straight into his eyes like I mean it. So far I haven't told a lie.

"It's funny we didn't find you," he says. "We drove all around."

28

1969

Olive's mum plonked the baby in the pram. He was teething and he had two hot, pink patches on his cheeks and would not stop wailing. She told us to take him for a walk around the square – no further – see if that settled him.

Olive got to do the pushing because he was her brother. He had on a blue-checked romper suit and his chubby legs were bare. The pram had a green canopy with a cream silk fringe that rippled as we went along. We sang "Ob-La-Di Ob-La-Da" to him and he stopped wailing, looked up at us like we were crazy. We wheeled him round and round the square, singing about Desmond and Molly Jones, till he shut his eyes and Olive had enough of pushing.

She stopped and put on the brake. "D'you want a shot?"

I looked in the pram. Bobby was dozing now and a bubble of snot was blowing in and out of his nose. I said, "It's okay."

"You'll have to do it someday," Olive said, "once you're married."

I didn't see why I had to get married. And she said, "Don't be daft. D'you want to be like June and be lonely all your life?"

It was the first time she'd said June's name out loud since she shut the door on us and I could tell it came out by accident because she clammed up as soon as she said it and didn't even try to contradict me when I said I reckoned married people could be lonely too. This thing with June hurt her worse than Vanessa not choosing her to sit with on the bus, a lot worse.

The baby stirred and she gave the pram a joggle, but he just started wailing and the bubble of snot burst and dribbled down into his mouth.

Olive said, "Shut up."

And he wailed louder.

She said shut up again and reached over the handlebar, smacked his bare leg hard. At first, he only looked surprised. His eyes went round and wide. And he shut up – just like that – held his breath till his face turned puce. Then he exploded and howled harder than ever.

I said, "What d'you hit him for?"

"It was only a tap. He has to learn." She shrugged like it was nothing but it was a slap I heard, and there were four red finger marks on his leg to prove it.

"He's not one of your dolls," I said.

And she snapped, "What's that supposed to mean?"

I didn't tell her. Olive's dolls never learned and she was always having to smack them. But dolls were dumb. They didn't howl like the baby. Plus doll skin didn't mark. We went round the square again singing "Ob-La-Di" at the top of our voices, drowning him out till he calmed down and went back to sleep. Then Olive wiped his nose and we took him home.

Peter was parked on the doorstep with his sketchpad, drawing another dinosaur. It had three horns, a stumpy one stuck on its nose and a long one above each eye. I asked what it was called and he said, "Triceratops." Just one word. A big one though and I was pleased to get that much out of him.

I told him his picture was good, and Olive said, "Don't encourage him. Ask him why he has to be so weird. Ask him why he can't draw something else, something normal, like a human being."

Peter made a face, as if a human being was a disgusting idea.

"You could do a horse," I said.

He cocked his head and looked up at me. I could tell he was interested in the horse idea. He didn't say anything though.

Olive lifted the baby out of the pram and he started to

snuffle again. She said to Peter, "Let us by." But he didn't budge. He bent over the sketchpad and started on another dinosaur, and she said, "Move it, weirdo. You're in the way."

Peter kept his head down and went on drawing, acting deaf as well as dumb and, next thing I knew, Olive shoved the baby into my arms. I'd never held a baby before. I didn't have a clue what to do with this hot, damp, scary bundle. She snatched Peter's sketchpad and tossed it in the air. It hovered above us for a moment, pages flapping, before it dived and crashed down on the path. She yanked at Peter's T-shirt and tried to drag him off the step.

The baby's snuffling got louder and he started squirming. He was getting hotter, heavier, damper, and I was scared I'd drop him. Peter jabbed his pencil into Olive's neck and I clutched the baby closer to me. She yelped and grabbed the pencil off him, snapped it in two. It looked to me like she was winning until Peter started smirking.

And Olive screamed, "What is it? WHAT?"

He took his time and smirked some more before he finally said, "I know where you go after school. I've seen you both."

29

1973

The police have gone – and Mum's too furious to sit down now. My eyes are getting sore from watching her pacing back and forth. The armchair still holds the sergeant's body heat and a lingering whiff of him. Old Spice. And fart. I have to clench my backside tight to stop myself sinking into the warm seat cushion.

She wants to know why I've been skipping school. She asks me over and over. And all I can say is – I don't know.

She doesn't believe me but it's true. My belly's turning somersaults and my head as well and I'm not sure of anything any more. At first I thought it was just about Olive – this need to go back to our old hiding places. Not that I wanted to find her. In fact, it was the opposite. I wanted to make sure she was gone. But this morning up at Pisgah Wood, when the fence got in my way, it was me that needed to get there, me that needed to melt into the shadows, disappear for a while, and when I started kicking it wasn't about Olive at all.

I still haven't done my maths homework yet, still can't get my head round cosines and tangents. I don't know how I'm supposed to concentrate with Mum and Dad at home and awake at the wrong times of day. Plus they're not speaking, not in front of me anyway, though I hear them in their room for hours.

She stops at the window for a second and gazes across the square in the direction of the Broadfoots' house. "I'm sick of all your secrecy, sick of you both, you and your dad." She starts to pace again. "D'you know where he is right now?"

I tell her I don't and she glares back at me. "Neither do I." As if this was my fault on top of everything else.

But her eyes are frantic and she's grey with exhaustion,

and she has to face the night shift next. The sergeant and Gulliver woke her early, and I do feel quite bad about that. The woman from the show house described me so well they knew it couldn't be anyone else. They checked with the school. They quizzed Claire. They left Mum waiting here to worry for hours about where I'd got to and whether I'd ever come back or if I'd vanish like Olive. And I know I should try to tell her I'm sorry but I can already guess what she'll say. Sorry isn't good enough. She always wants more out of me than I give, and I can never work out how much will be enough for her and not too much for me. I don't even try now.

And where is Dad when she needs him anyway? I say, "He'll be home soon." Say it like I'm sure.

She gives up pacing and sinks down on the couch. "D'you think so?"

I nod – and she suddenly looks so crumpled and small. Everything about her seems to have shrunk, except for her eyes which are bigger than ever, huge green pools of pain and fear. I tell her not to worry and that I'm not worried either, though really I'm out of my depth. And I tell her like I mean it, "He'll be back for dinner." Though I don't think he'll be expecting food. These last few days, every dinner has been a disaster, undercooked, overcooked, burnt beyond recognition, hours late, or forgotten altogether, and we're all getting thinner.

"I've got nothing in," she says now. "You better run to the butcher's."

It's only ten minutes till closing time and I'll have to hurry if I want to get there before they pull down the shutters. She digs her purse out of her handbag and hands me the money.

"A pound of best minced beef," she says. "A quarter pound per head and a quarter for the pot."

She says the same thing every time, chants it like some kind of spell, some witchy wisdom, some meaty secret mothers must pass on to daughters, and every time I hear "a quarter for the pot" it makes me grin inside and I picture a bubbling cauldron slurping down its share.

I get up to leave and she says, "Don't forget the change."

Of course, I know what she actually means is *don't spend it… don't steal it*. I give her a hurt look as if to say I've grown out of that, which is almost true as long as you don't count Dad's cigarettes.

She calls after me, "Come straight back." But I'm in the hall now and don't bother to answer. I can't wait to get out the door.

My legs are stiff and my feet feel like two dead weights, but there's no time to dawdle. I won't make it unless I run all the way. At first, I have to force myself to move but the more I run the more I want to run and my feet feel lighter and lighter the farther I get from home. Muscles loosen off and I don't want to stop. I want to keep running all the way to the edge of the world, and not stop there either, gallop off into empty space where there is no resistance.

The butcher's already putting the meat away when I burst in, panting. He sighs and says, "No trouble." Though it clearly is.

I say sorry, and thank you, and sorry again. The reek of dead flesh makes me dizzy, and I gaze out through the open door into the fresh clean air while he slaps the bloody mound of mince on to the scales. He stuffs it into a brown paper bag, and I hand over the money and thank him again. The coins he hands me back in change carry the scent of blood transferred from his fingers and I pocket them quickly and wipe my hand on my skirt.

Mum said to come straight back but I can't face going home yet. I don't want to find out if Dad's there and I don't want to find out he's not. Either way, she won't be happy. Either way, I'll be stuck in the middle. I decide to ignore the "straight" bit and set off the roundabout way down by the river. The path is rutted from last winter's flood when the river broke its banks and bit chunks out of the ground. I have to watch where I step. But the water is low now, the sound of it soothing. I stop halfway across the footbridge and light a cigarette, lean over the railing and peer down into the dark water, catch the flickers of small darting fish. I wish Mum could see a band's not so bad. It doesn't have to be her or them, and I know she would never understand this, but I'm scared she'll make him choose and he'll choose her. Choose us. Let his chance go. Because how can he go on dreaming then? And why should his secret audience go on listening? Who would he be without them?

This cigarette was the last in the pack and I drag on it more deeply than usual and it burns down faster, and I think I should quit after this one. Quit smoking. Quit stealing. Maybe I will. The idea seems easier with the sound of the river washing through me, possible at least.

The cigarette is almost done, just one more drag to go when I hear the dogs barking and a wolf whistle leaps through the air. I turn and see Tony's two Alsatians tearing along the riverbank ahead of him. He's not a boy any more, and not a man yet either. Hair still the colour of caramel, but longer now, curling over his collar, falling over one eye. Still too thin, but his shoulders are broader and squarer and, as he gets closer, I remember how weirdly out of proportion his head used to be. It looks okay these days.

He tries to call the dogs back but they keep tearing on. They charge on to the bridge and he starts to run. His yells cut through the soft damp air. The dogs are almost on me before they finally obey. They rear up barely a foot away, thick necks straining towards the poke of mince and the smell of blood. I stuff the poke inside my jacket and Tony comes up behind them and says hi. I say nothing back. I don't even look at him – just stand there with the cigarette burning down between my fingertips, transfixed by the dogs' throbbing jaws, bared teeth, steaming tongues.

He strolls between them now, hands in pockets, grinning, and says, "D'you know who I am?"

And I think – what sort of weird question is that? Apart from that time at the NAAFI, I've never had to speak to him, and I'm not going to say his name out loud now just for his benefit. I just nod.

"So why d'you always act like you've never met me before?" He's grinning at me still, and I want to tell him to get lost and I've no idea what he means. But he gets in first and takes the smouldering cigarette end from me, tosses it in the river, says, "It doesn't suit you."

And I don't have a clue what's coming next till he moves in and kisses me. And I think this is a Cowboy Kiss, and all I have to do is resist. Or I could kiss him back, but I'm not sure how. And I wonder what Olive would do. Would she stick to the rules? Would she even remember the three kinds of kissing now? And he stops and tells me to open my lips, and I let his tongue in, and the river swims beneath our feet, and I can't make up my mind if I like it or not, and I wonder if he's getting bored yet, and the mince is getting squashed, and the dogs are panting over his shoulders, hot stinking breath, and he stops again and barks, "DOWN."

This is my chance. I pull away and say, "I have to go now." I don't look back, just run and run all the way home.

30

1969

Mid-June – and my days of walking to school with Olive were almost done. Come the autumn term, she'd be off on the high-school bus before I even had breakfast. It was time I got used to the idea. That morning when I got to the Broadfoots' gate, I thought about going on by to see what it felt like and, while I was swithering, their door opened and Peter Broadfoot stared out at me. He had on his shoes and school blazer ready to go, plus his cap gun in a holster slung low on his hips. I said hello, and he said nothing back.

I tried again. "Is Olive ready?"

He fingered the butt of his gun and went on staring. Most boys were weird in my opinion, not quite human, but Peter Broadfoot was the weirdest, an alien beamed here from some distant planet where silence reigned and giant lizards roamed.

Olive came thudding down the stairs behind him and called out to me, "I'm not late. You're early. Move it, Squirt." She pushed past Peter and skipped down the steps.

Most mornings, he left the square in the opposite direction from us, out on to William Street. He didn't like to be seen with Olive and she felt the same. But that morning he trailed close behind us through the lane past the Doig's white rabbits, whistling the *Bonanza* theme tune, and Olive kept hissing *shut up, shut up*. In Springfield Road, he drew his cap gun and took aim.

BANG

"You're dead."

Just two words but a lot for him. I whipped around in time to see a puff of smoke rising from the muzzle of his gun, caught a whiff of sulphur. His eyes narrowed to vicious slits and he aimed again. The bang cracked through the air and crows took off from the rooftops squawking and wheeling in the blue sky. I ducked behind the nearest car and fired my imaginary pistol back.

KAPOW

"Don't encourage him," Olive said and stormed on ahead. I pretended I didn't hear.

BANG

KAPOW

BANG

KAPOW

We kept the gunfire going past the red phone box and on to the railway bridge. Olive was waiting for me at the far end, fuming. "Don't you know what he's up to? Whose side are you on?" She glanced towards the entrance to the alley and back at me. "Ignore him, okay?"

I nodded. But my finger stayed crooked around my imaginary trigger. We couldn't go in the alley with him on our tail. We had to lead him the long way round by Station Road and past the post office. For a while, the bangs kept coming and I had to stop myself from firing back. Then maybe he ran out of caps, or maybe he just got fed up and decided to save what he had left. But anyway, we walked the rest of the way in silence. At the school gates, we hung back for a bit and watched him stroll by. He was whistling the *Bonanza* theme tune again, flat and lagging behind the beat.

Olive said, "He's not as dumb as everybody thinks, you know."

I frowned after him. It was hard to tell.

In class, I kept an eye on him. I wasn't sure what I was looking for exactly. Something different. Something to prove Olive was right. But there was nothing. He was his usual dumb self. The substitute teacher asked the name of Apollo 10's lunar module and he was the only one who didn't put up his hand. Of course, this only drew the teacher's attention to him, the opposite of what he wanted, more proof he was dumb.

She said, "Come on, Peter, I think you know perfectly well."

But Billy Cairns couldn't wait. He shouted out, "Snoopy," and she never found out if Peter really knew or not.

*

After school that afternoon, he was close behind us again when we got to the high street. We stopped to look in the chemist shop window and waited for him to pass. The loofahs and long-handled brushes for scrubbing backs always made us shudder, and we both coveted the Hartnell *in Love* talcum powder in the pink plastic heart-shaped dispenser. But right then we were more interested in watching for Peter's reflection. He turned his head as he went by and peered over our shoulders into the glass, smirking to himself.

Olive hissed, "Get lost." And his smirk turned into a snigger.

He stopped at the next shop window and waited for us to move on. It served him right that it was the undertaker's and he had to stand there looking at gravestones. We raced past him and kept running all the way down to the bottom of the high street and on to the road bridge. If we were quick, we could maybe slip into the alley without him seeing. The river rushed beneath our feet and our lungs were pumping hard. We were nearly there – but when we looked back he was already starting on to the bridge.

We stopped at the bottom of the alley and Olive said we had to get rid of him. She didn't say how though, and I had no idea. My belly was rumbling and all I could think of was her grandma's scones waiting for us, warm and golden on the outside, butter melting in the middle. Peter slowed down and swaggered towards us, one hand on his gun, the other in his trouser pocket. Smirking still. Olive was right. He wasn't as dumb as folk thought. There was a sneaky side to him.

I said, "Let's go and see your grandma anyway. He can't prove anything. Your mum can ask me if she doesn't believe you, and I'll say he's a liar."

Olive just said, "I'll kill him."

He came right up to her now. Too close for me to get in between. Not that I wanted to anyway. I knew when to stay out of it.

Olive said, "Get lost, weirdo." And it was a stand-off now, a staring competition. Peter's eyes were hard and Olive's eyes were snapping.

I said, "I'm going," and they just went on trying to outstare each other like they hadn't heard.

I walked away and left them to it. I knew how it would end. Their fights always went the same way. Olive would lash out first but she couldn't win. She could beat him black and blue and Peter would still smirk. I was almost at the post office before I heard the wallop and the yelp. I didn't turn to look. I was glad to be out of it, and I was past the station before it dawned on me I didn't need to go the long way round. I could cut through the alley any time I liked. It wasn't up to Olive's mum, or Peter, or anybody else.

31

1973

Mum wants to know – right now – how the mince poke got in such a state, burst on both sides, oozing blood. And I've got no choice but to lie and tell her I dropped it on the ground. She frowns at the ripped brown paper bag sitting on the kitchen counter. "So how did you manage to drop it exactly?" As if there might be umpteen ways to drop a pound of mince.

I tell her it slipped – that's all. This seems fair enough to me but she says, "It looks like you did more than drop it."

I don't know what she thinks I did with it. Punch it? Kick it? Throw it about? Or what? "It rolled a bit," I say.

But she's still not happy. "Rolled?" she says. "D'you think I'm daft?"

She leans forward, peers at me, and I smell the sherry on her breath. I glance around the kitchen. No sign of the bottle anywhere. No sign of a glass. But I'm sure all the same. I can always tell from her eyes – the way they can suddenly go misty and distant.

Lost for a moment.

Like now.

And then – they change back again, go sharp and clear. They can still do that, in an instant, pierce right through you before you've time to get your guard up.

"So how exactly did it roll?" she says. As if mince might roll umpteen ways.

I tell her, "It was on that steep bit in William Street."

And she explodes. "I didn't ask you *where*. I want you to explain to me how the hell this mince managed to defy the laws of physics. It doesn't matter how steep the hill is, mince just wouldn't roll."

"Look." She snatches the torn, bloody poke from the counter. Holds it out at arm's length.

Lets go.

It plummets SPLAT and flattens on to the kitchen floor and globs of pink, glistening, flesh bulge through the ragged tears. I check her face to see if I'm supposed to laugh. But no – she starts snapping now. "Why d'you always have something to hide? Why can't you just be honest for once?" She glares at me.

I look away, stare down at the mince. I can't tell her about Tony but even if I could I don't think she'd believe a kiss could do this much damage.

"It's the secrecy I don't understand," she says. "This stupid, stubborn secrecy."

I cringe when she says *secrecy*, hate the way she makes it hiss. I clamp my teeth together, cage my tongue, look back at her defiantly.

"Go on," she says. "Get out of my sight."

I stamp out of the kitchen and up the stairs, slam the bathroom door and draw the bolt behind me. Safe. I turn on the cold tap full blast for the noise, a gushing wall between us now. I study the face in the mirror.

Me.

But not the me I'm used to – strange new flecks of light in the eyes, lips all rosy and swollen. I wonder if this is how Tony sees me. I hope so. I can't decide if I like him or not, but I want him to like me. I didn't ask to be kissed, but it better mean something. It better not be some kind of a joke. There are so many things I don't know how to say yet, even to myself, never mind anyone else, feelings I don't have the words for. I know what Olive would say though. I can almost hear her, almost feel her breath brushing the rim of my ear – *You can't trust any kind of kissing. It never means what it's supposed to mean.*

Dad comes home whistling, in time for dinner. I hear him through my bedroom window as he comes up the front path. He sounds hopeful. I don't know why. He's still in her black books. We both are. But it feels easier now he's here, his turn to worry about Mum for a while.

The kitchen door is open when I get downstairs and I stop and watch them from the hall – standing at the cooker close together, wreathed in the vapours of sizzling mince and onions. I can't see her face, only his, smiling and frowning both at once. How does he manage that? It looks painful. He dips his head towards her now, goes to kiss her, and she lets him. I wasn't sure she would and he looks relieved – grateful – though she doesn't kiss him back. And I think of the rules for a Serious Kiss, and I'm scared she can't kiss back because it doesn't feel true. I wish she would try though, pretend if she has to and give him a chance, stop making all of us suffer. Because it was true not so long ago. It's been true all my life, and she can't just stop loving him now.

He murmurs something I can't make out and she seems to be listening. That's a good sign at least. Maybe we'll eat later or maybe not and the dinner will end up in the bin again. Either way, he still has a lot of persuading to do. I tiptoe back upstairs to my room and let them get on with it. They need to try harder, but who's going to tell them?

I fumble in my pocket and pull out the cigarette packet. Empty. Giving up doesn't seem like such a good idea now. I don't know what else to do with myself, and I still can't face trigonometry. I turn on the radio, catch a snatch of Elton John and "Rocket Man" and switch it off again. I need to hear what's happening downstairs.

I go to the window and check the Broadfoots' house. Their windows glare back at me. Maybe it's weird but I don't trust their windows. There has always been something impossible to believe about the Broadfoots' place, the too-neat garden, the pristine paintwork, and I've been inside often enough to know there's no mess there either. At least, not the kind of mess you can see. No dustballs gathering in the corner. No dirty dishes piled up in the sink. Not like ours. But there's another kind of mess even Gina Broadfoot can't control no matter how hard she scrubs and nags. Peter is gone and now Olive too, and she'll never know why.

32

1969

Every day after school, we tried to get back to the alley. And every day Peter was on our tail with his cap gun in his holster. Never too close, he always kept a few steps behind us. He didn't want to look like he was with us but he wanted us to know he was there. We tried to shake him off but running from him didn't work. We tried leading him the longest, twistiest ways home in the hope that he'd lose interest, through the churchyard, weaving in among the gravestones, through the goods yard behind the railway station, round and round the grid of streets that framed the square. And still he stuck with us.

Olive was getting desperate to see her grandma again and she was scared the Lord might not go on sparing her. He might not wait till we got rid of Peter. I didn't miss her grandma so much, or her custard creams, but I did miss her scones. Our walks home from school were blistered with bangs from Peter's cap gun. It got on Olive's nerves but I kind of liked it. One time, I even bought a roll of caps and lobbed it to him so he could keep the gunfire going.

Olive said, "Why d'you encourage him?" And I shrugged and said sorry.

"Sorry isn't good enough," she said like she was my mum or something.

We got to the bottom end of the alley and, instead of going on by, she swung round and yelled, "Get lost, weirdo. You can't come."

He yelled back, "You can't go then." And I butted in, "Do you even care? I mean, do you really want to see where your grandma lives?"

He nodded and looked me straight in the eye. He didn't do that often, and I believed him but Olive said, "No way."

*

Peter didn't only muck up weekdays. He mucked up weekends as well and we had to stay away from the island, and the empty NAAFI, and the den in Pisgah Wood. If he got to know our hiding places, they'd never feel safe again. By the second Saturday, we were fed up running from him, and yelling did no good, and we decided we'd try boring him away instead. We paraded up and down the bright side of the high street till our legs ached and Olive got a knot in the middle of her forehead. She claimed it had nothing to do with Peter, and nothing to do with the sun in her eyes, and no we didn't need to cross to the shady side of the street. And she tried to tell me it had nothing to do with Lizzie's either, nothing to do with June. As if I couldn't see the way she sped up and turned her face away every time we passed the salon window and how her cheeks burned.

We stopped at the drinking fountain at the foot of the high street and Olive dipped her head to the spurt of water while Peter prowled past, smirking again.

I said, "Are you worried he'll tell? About your grandma, I mean."

Olive wiped her mouth and looked up at me. "He never tells. That would take too many words. It's silent threats with him."

"So what are you so worried about then?"

The knot in her forehead got tighter. "Who says I am?"

"You're frowning," I said. Nobody frowned that hard for nothing. I knew that much at least.

She pressed her palms into her belly. "I've got cramps. Okay? Plus backache. D'you know what I'm on about?"

I said, "Oh that."

"It'll be your turn soon," she said.

I didn't want to talk about it. Soon wasn't yet, and I didn't want to think about my body changing, not until I had to. It felt fine the way it was. It fitted me at least. Unlike Olive's body – which nipped and squeezed and made her snappy.

On the far side of the road bridge, Peter was skulking behind a red van parked outside the post office, watching to see which way we went next.

"Look at him," I said to her. "What'll he do if we stay here? We could make him wait."

Olive agreed that it was worth a try and we moved to sit on the bench by the fountain. The slats on the seat were warm from the sun and, for a while, we didn't say anything, just sat and watched him watching us. Every time he moved his head, the sunlight caught in his hair and made it glint like copper. He hadn't actually said he would tell on us but then he never said much. He could be *thinking* anything though, creepy stuff, crazy stuff, and we would never know. He couldn't always be thinking about dinosaurs. Maybe he had other monsters.

I said to Olive, "If you're so sure he won't tell, why d'you let him stop us going to see your grandma? Why don't we just let him come with us?"

She squished up her face like she was in pain and the knot in the middle of her forehead bulged. "You've got it the wrong way round. I'm the one stopping him. He's not lucky like me. He always manages to get caught in the end and, if we take him with us, he'll get us caught as well."

It was the first I knew Olive believed she was lucky.

33

Gonnella's Café has dark wood-panelled walls, grim as a funeral parlour. We wouldn't come here if we had a choice but the other cafés don't allow underage smokers, plus they don't have a jukebox. Claire and I rush to bag the best seats at the far end from the door, backs to the wall, where we can see who comes and goes without turning our heads. We wouldn't want to look like we're interested. That would not be cool.

But it's impossible to look cool today anyway, not with Morag Ross crouched across the table from us like a giant mouse – Claire's idea, not mine. She mumbles the odd word to Claire, but nothing to me, and she hasn't once looked me straight in the eye. You'd think I was scary or something. Right now she's gazing over my shoulder at the deathly dark wall, and it's starting to piss me off. In fact, I can't stand to look at her either and I could do with a cigarette to take my mind off her. Claire hasn't even noticed I quit yet. We could've gone somewhere else for lunch. There's a lot I haven't got round to telling her lately. Like the fact I've got a job and my dad lost his. And I'm not even tempted to tell her about Tony. I should've slapped him. If it happened to Claire, that's what I'd say to her. You shouldn't just let him.

She says to Morag now, "You can come with us again tomorrow if you like, and the next day, in fact any time. You don't have to eat on your own."

Morag nods shyly.

And I'm pissed off with Claire as well now. The thought of Morag every day is too much. She should've asked if it was okay with me first. She starts to tell us about some Monty Python sketch she saw last night on telly. A highwayman steals lupins from the rich and tries to give them to the poor. Morag pretends she gets it but her eyes are vacant, and it doesn't sound all that funny to me.

Claire says, "You'd have to see it."

I just raise my eyebrows and fidget with the ashtray till the waitress gets to us. We order chips and buttered rolls, and Claire and Morag ask for Cokes. I don't have the money to pay for a drink and Claire asks for an extra straw so we can both sip from her glass. She's good that way, good in a lot of ways really. I'm not so sure she'd say the same about me though.

She pokes her head towards Morag now. "Tell Grace what you told me about Olive outside your house in the dark."

And Morag looks at me at last. Just for a second. Looks away fast. Her chin retreats into her neck and she works her lips from side to side, like she's gathering her words together. I sprinkle salt over my chips and throw on some vinegar, and "All Along the Watchtower" starts playing on the jukebox.

Finally Morag says, "It seems like a dream now."

I stab my fork into a chip. "Maybe it was. A dream, I mean. Maybe you were seeing things."

"Don't listen to her," Claire says. "She's been in a mood for days. I believe you anyway."

I shrug. Claire can believe what she likes. I say to Morag, "How come you're so sure it was Olive? It was dark. It could've been anyone."

She blinks at me. "But there was the streetlight. I could make out the shape and there was her shadow on the pavement. I've seen her shadow before, loads of times."

And I think this is getting ridiculous. First, it's a dream. Now it's a shadow. Maybe Morag just wants some attention. "So what are you telling us for? Why don't you tell the police?"

She blinks again. "Would you?"

"We'd have to tell them," Claire says, "for Olive's own good."

I bet she would as well. Claire always tries to do the right thing. This doesn't mean she always knows what the right thing is though, and she doesn't know Olive at all. Morag understands it's complicated at least. Not that this means we're on the same side. It doesn't make us friends or anything.

I lean across the table towards her now, shut Claire out. "I wouldn't tell anyone, not even you."

*

On the bus home, Claire gets on ahead of me and goes to sit with Morag. No explanation, just leaves me alone, up on the top deck right at the front with the hum of disembodied voices behind me and the grey road streaming ahead. I try not to care but I can't get the empty seat out of my mind. It's bad enough that Claire's deserted me, for Morag Ross of all people, but that's not all that's bothering me. It's like the space on the bus where Olive used to be has shifted two seats forward to be next to me. And the sense of her absence is so strong I can't bear to look. I stare through the window all the way home, stare straight ahead as hard as I can till the world outside blurs and it starts to feel as if I'm vanishing as well, and there are two empty seats at the front of the bus now.

*

I get back to the square in time to see Bill Broadfoot trudging down our garden path, and Mum at the front door watching him go. He's in his slippers, red-and-gold tartan, and she's still in her dressing gown. I wish she'd get back inside, put some proper clothes on. The dressing gown is embarrassing enough but his slippers make it look worse, too intimate, indecent somehow. When he gets to me, he stops and lifts his head, looks me deep in the eyes. I get the feeling he doesn't really see me though. He's too busy looking for somebody else.

He clears his throat as if he is about to speak but,

before he can say a word, Mum calls out, "Leave it, Bill."
A warning note in her voice but gentle with it, as if she
wishes she didn't have to say it. He nods. To me, I think,
though maybe more for her benefit. She disappears into
the house and I give him an awkward half-smile and slip
past him.

I find her hovering at the living room window, still
watching him go. I say hello and she sighs. "The police are
saying there's nothing more they can do. No suspicious
circumstances as far as they can see, just a simple runaway.
But it's never simple, is it?"

I don't know how to answer. No one ever vanished on
me before.

She turns to look at me. "He thought you might have heard
from her. You haven't, have you? That's what I told him."

I tell her no. This is not a lie but it feels nothing like the
truth. She seems happy with it though. I don't think she
really wanted to hear anything else. No dream shadow
on the pavement. No hint that Olive's leaving could
have anything to do with me. I can't believe she doesn't
suspect though. She usually suspects. She's suspicious
by nature, just like I am secretive. You could say we
deserve each other in a weird sort of way, and we can
make each other worse sometimes. But there's no sherry
on her breath today. Her eyes are clear, and she even
smiles now, only a small smile but the first one in days.
She says, "I thought maybe we could go and see this band
your dad didn't want us to know about. They've got a gig
tomorrow night."

I start to grin. "Does he know we're coming?"

"Not yet. I thought we could surprise him."

I think about the last time we tried to surprise him,
the cobwebs clinging to the lintel of Gordon Brothers'
Engineering, the buzzer drilling through abandoned offices.
Surprises can backfire.

"You don't have to come," she says, "only if you want."

152

But nothing would keep me away. I ask her where, and what time. And does this mean she'll give him and the band a chance.

She says, "He's had a lot of chances." And I picture the woman with the blue guitar case.

34

1969

The rain always poured when we didn't want it. First day of the summer holidays – and it was battering down when I let Olive into the house. We went to the kitchen and raided the biscuit tin, and she wolfed down three digestives in the time it took me to eat one. Plus she still managed to do all the talking. She said she could only stay a minute. Her mum wanted her back home to help with the cleaning. She had all the skirting boards to wipe and the handles on every single door and drawer. With disinfectant – she hated the smell. Peter, of course, didn't have to do anything because he was a boy. It was enough to make you sick and I was lucky I didn't have a brother. Peter never had to lift a finger. She said we'd have to lose him later. We didn't want him on our tails ruining another day. She told me where to meet her. And still she didn't leave.

She hung back rubbing her head, and I guessed before she let me see. She'd had bumps on the head before, but nobody saw because of her hair. I was the only one who knew and I wasn't supposed to tell. She said if I did she'd send me to Coventry. Nobody spoke to people in Coventry and they deserved it, Olive said, because they were not good friends.

This time it happened because she spilled cornflakes and her mum thumped her head off the kitchen wall. I said, "Cornflakes isn't that bad."

Olive said, "It is to her. Milk and mush all over her clean floor."

The bump on her head looked like a wee bluebird's egg nesting in her hair. I was scared to touch it but she promised me it wouldn't break. She grabbed my hand and pressed my fingers in until her eyes began to glitter and go red around the rims. She said it happened all the time. People got hurt in places that didn't show. She needed somebody else to know – to make it real, make it true. But she was glad it was only me. She wouldn't want anyone else feeling sorry for her – and especially not Vanessa or Patsy or any of the new girls. It was okay to show me because I lived where she lived, in the same kind of house. Plus I already knew what her mum was like.

*

The Broadfoots' shed was hidden behind an ivy-covered trellis at the end of their back garden. We had loads of hideouts but this one was the easiest to get to in a hurry. You could get there by the lanes that ran behind the square and no one in the Broadfoots' house would spot you sneaking in. Our shed only had a padlock, but the Broadfoots' had a proper lock and key that you could turn from the inside so no one could come barging in. There was no window for folk to spy on us. Folk like Peter and Olive's mum. And it didn't matter that we couldn't see out. The crunchy gravel path outside meant no one could creep up and take us by surprise. It still didn't feel safe though. Hiding places never did. Just the fact we were hiding was enough to give us the jitters.

It was still raining when I got there. And it was dark inside. But not the kind of dark you saw when you shut your eyes. That wasn't really dark at all. Here is something Olive taught me: you shut your eyes and screwed them up tight until you saw wee dots of light. Once you knew how you could make the dots do things by squeezing your eyes different ways. You could make them dance and change colour, or let them drift like balloons. Or you could take a tiny dot of light and make it grow until there was no darkness left.

I was first there – as usual. I always had to wait. Olive would never admit it but she was scared of being alone in the dark and there was always something stopped her getting there before me, some feeble excuse I was supposed to believe. I never let on if I did or I didn't.

The dark inside the shed was stuffy and more brown than black. I breathed in the smell of musty wood and oil and potting compost while my eyes got used to it. And the rain pattered down on the tin roof till bit by bit the fuzzy shapes of garden tools began to appear – and Bill Broadfoot's big black bicycle. I dragged a metal box alongside it and clambered on to the saddle to wait. My hands didn't reach the handlebars and it was wobbly up there. Every couple of minutes, I had to jump down to give my backside a rest.

We used to come here more often and Olive used to bring a torch but then her brother started nosing about and we didn't come so much any more and we stopped bringing the torch because there was this wee crack down near the bottom of the door. You wouldn't notice the light unless you looked hard. Peter might look hard though, and once he knew we were inside, he'd want to know what we were up to. We used to practise Cowboy Kissing there but now we had to wait till we were up in Pisgah Wood. Olive said we needed to practise so we got it right when it came to the real thing. She was getting really good at resisting but she slapped too hard and then she wanted to do it again. It stung even worse when she used water for the whisky and flung it in my face, and I was getting fed up with being the cowboy.

When she finally showed up, she slipped in fast. A sliver of light for a split second. Then darkness again. I heard the key scrape in the lock and caught a whiff of disinfectant.

"Hello."

She sounded funny when I couldn't see her face, kind of snuffly and faraway, and I had to concentrate on what she was saying.

"Sorry I'm late. I couldn't come with Peter watching." All I could see of her was a black shadow shifting in the brown darkness.

"How's your head?"

She said, "Throbbing."

I pictured the wee blue egg pulsating, getting ready to hatch.

She said, "I don't want to stay here. It's too close to home."

"Where d'you want to go then?"

"How should I know?" Her voice hissed back at me through the darkness. "Anywhere but here, as far away from *her* as I can get, and Peter too, from both of them."

But it was pouring outside and I wasn't keen on leaving yet. We took it in turns to perch on the saddle while we waited for a break in the rain. And Olive said she was my best friend and I could trust her. She wasn't sure she could trust me though. Sometimes, she thought I wasn't a good friend because I never told her anything. I must have a secret, maybe something to do with my mum, something she wouldn't want Olive or anyone knowing.

She said, "Nobody's mum is perfect."

But I couldn't think of any secrets.

"So your mum's perfect?" Olive said. Though I never claimed she was. "She must be," Olive said. "Perfect."

There was no point in trying to argue with her when she was in this kind of mood. She would just keep on and on. I said, "So how many handles are there in your house. Did you count them?"

She hadn't thought of counting them but she started to work it out in her head now. She went over every handle on every door and every drawer in every room. The tap-tapping of the rain on the tin roof got lighter and lighter and she was still counting and I wished I'd never asked.

"Seventy-three," she said in the end.

"Is that all?" Considering how long it took her to count them, this didn't seem that many to me. "What about the one for flushing the toilet? Did you remember it?"

Olive sighed and her warm breath wafted through the darkness. "Okay, seventy-four but I forgot to wipe that one."

"Think of the germs." I started to giggle.

And she joined in. "They'll be spreading all over the house."

"Coming to get us," I said back.

She jumped down from the saddle. "We better get out of here now."

We slipped the key under the brick behind the shed and dived through the back lanes, splashing through puddles, surfaced in William Street, free. The sun came out and shone on the drizzle, filling the air with flickering drops of light. We didn't know where we were going yet. Well, I didn't anyway – and Olive didn't say. We drifted through the shimmering drizzle and she didn't mention her grandma once. We didn't even bother to look out for Peter. It felt good not having to think about either of them, the most relaxed in days.

But of course Olive hadn't really forgotten her grandma or Peter. That was only me. She knew where she was going. We ended up at the top of the alley as usual, and when we looked back, there was Peter on the railway bridge. All we could see was the top of his head bobbing above the parapet but we were sure it was him all the same. That bristly, strawberry blond hair couldn't belong to anybody else.

Olive yelled, "Get lost, Peter." And he ducked. She yelled again, "We know you're there," and started back towards the bridge. She said to me, "I'm going to throttle him."

But I was fed up with all their battling. I didn't see the point. It didn't make him go away. I said, "He won't give in. You always hurt him worse than he hurts you and it never stops him coming back to bug us."

"So what are we supposed to do then?"

"Go to the park. Let him come if he wants. We'll ignore him."

She looked at me like I was crazy. "You can ignore him if you like. I'm still going to throttle him."

"Okay, but throttle him later." I turned and set off down the orange chip path behind the signal box towards the west bank of the river and Olive trailed after me, moaning. "He wouldn't have the time to bug us if he had any friends. But who would want to hang around with him? The dumb boy? He *thinks* plenty of stuff, you know."

I didn't answer, just walked faster. It felt the wrong way round somehow, me leading. I hardly ever went first. I looked back over my shoulder. "We've got a head start on him."

Olive grinned and nodded, and we took off and raced full pelt along the bank. The roar of the river drowned out our footsteps and our huffing and puffing as well. The water was higher than it had been in weeks, and the rubble causeway to our island had vanished, sunk below foamy Coca-Cola-coloured water.

35

1973

The city heat hits us when we step off the train at Queen Street, and straight away Mum's make-up starts to melt and give her skin a clammy, feverish sheen. She has on a sleeveless shift, the same sea green as her eyes, and clip-on pearly earrings that pinch at her lobes.

We stop at the traffic lights and she rubs one ear then the other. "It's not far," she says. "But we're early. Your dad says there's a restaurant next door."

"So does he know we're coming then?" The woman with the blue guitar case has been on my mind all the way here – and how this surprise could go wrong.

"Not for sure," Mum says. "He's hoping."

The lights change and I smile at the thought of him hoping as we cross the road.

*

The Dial Inn restaurant has telephones on every table. We've never been anywhere like it before and, at first, we're not sure we should stay. We passed a Wimpy Bar on the way. We'd know what we're getting there at least. The resident DJ's voice warbles through the speakers, calling for requests and urging us to pick up our phones.

Mum says, "You should." But I'm not keen. I only want live music tonight.

You have to phone your orders for food and drink as well. We decide on Caesar salads and Mum dials for service. It should be simple but she manages to spin it out, asking who she's speaking to and where they are. Not in the kitchen, apparently. Finally, she says, "Oh, and we'll have a bottle of the Asti Spumante." As if she'd nearly forgotten – I look away from the table and hope she can see I'm not happy.

The restaurant's half-empty and all the other tables are couples, her age or older. Dad should be here with her, not me. The DJ puts on Neil Diamond and the man at the next table leans towards his plump wife and starts to croon "Sweet Caroline". She purses her lips and looks away, catches me watching them. Her eyes flick past me, as if I don't count, and fix on Mum. Maybe she's wondering what she's doing out without a man – or deciding who needs to lose the most weight. Mum does that sometimes.

The wine arrives and I frown at the bottle. "You're not going to drink all of it, are you?"

"I thought you could have a wee drop."

I glance after the waiter's retreating back and she says, "It's allowed."

"That's not what I meant."

"I know." She tilts the bottle to my glass and pours till it's half-full.

"I won't like it."

"Nobody does at first."

I let the glass lie while we wait for the food, but I can smell the wine already, rotten and sweet and stomach-churning. Even the name is disgusting. Asti Spumante. Nasty Spew. Mum takes a sip and puts her glass down, picks it up again a moment later, takes a slug and holds on to it this time, so tight her knuckles shine.

"So how's Claire doing?" she says.

I shrug. "Okay. Why?"

"Well, she *is* your best friend these days."

I know Mum's only looking for something to say but I wish she'd pick on something else. Claire sat with Morag again on the bus today and I gazed out the window till that vanishing feeling came back again. I don't want to talk about Claire, not to Mum, not to anybody, and I'm relieved when the Caesar salads arrive.

Mum says, "She's nice enough but you have to admit she

doesn't have Olive's spark. I never understood why you two fell out after Peter…"

The word she doesn't say hovers like a ghost in the air between us. Not that I believe in ghosts, unless a ghost is just a memory you picture back to life. Olive believed in them though, and she was scared of the dark as well. One time, she told me when the dark came down at night she got this smothering feeling, like she was being buried alive. I told her she was crazy.

"But we didn't fall out," I say to Mum now. And this is kind of true. It wasn't like we had a fight or anything. We just couldn't bear to look at each other any more, too scared of what we'd see, the secret in each other's eyes.

Mum drains her glass and pours another one, tops up mine while she's about it, and the bubbles sparkle and fizz. I haven't touched mine yet and now it's three quarters full. I screw up my face and take a tiny sip.

"You'll get used to it," she says.

I don't think I want to. "How long till the band's on?"

She glances at her wristwatch. "About half an hour."

"So what's their name?"

"Don't you know?" Her eyebrows go up. "I thought you would've asked him. Why didn't you?"

I shrug and crunch into a crouton. It's been hard to even look at him the last few days.

"They're called Take Five after that Dave Brubeck tune and because there's five of them." She rolls her eyes.

She never quite admits it but she's not crazy about jazz, doesn't have the patience for it when he wanders off the melody and he takes ages to come back. But she should know by now he always does. You just have to trust him. Let him take you on a mystery trip. There's not much point in us coming out tonight if she won't try a bit of trust. I've almost finished my salad and she's hardly started hers. She drains her glass again, like it was lemonade, and reaches for the bottle.

I say, "You should eat first." I know that much at least.

She starts to pour anyway. "I haven't any appetite. It's this Glasgow heat." But the restaurant is air-conditioned and she has goosebumps on her arms. She tilts the bottle to my glass, still three quarters full, and starts to top it up again, says, "We should be going next door soon."

The wine's brimming over the rim of my glass now, spilling on to the snowy tablecloth, and she keeps pouring. I try to take the bottle from her, and she snatches it away, plonks it down on her side of the table and shoots me an offended glare, as if the spreading patch of slush has nothing to do with her.

That look always used to be enough to convince me she must be right, but not this time. I glare straight back. "Maybe we should just go home." I wonder how long till the next train out of Glasgow. The couple at the next table are staring, the man curious and his plump wife purse-lipped. I'm not sure which is worse.

"But we've come all this way," Mum says. "And he'll be looking for us."

She dabs at the sodden tablecloth with her napkin and I sigh. "Okay, we'll stay but don't drink any more." And I want to add – *ever. Not another drop ever*. It's teetering on the tip of my tongue but we have to get through tonight.

*

In the Heidi Lounge, a fog of cigarette smoke, kid-on rustic tables and an orangey pine-clad ceiling, more men than women, a sea of men, beery breath, beery sweat, and Mum in her fresh sea green dress weaving her way through them to the bar. She seems to be the only woman buying her own drink. And I'm not the only one watching her. They look up from their pints and gaze after her. One man, two men, I stop counting after three. I wonder if she feels them watching. And does she mind? Is she as embarrassed as me? It's weird seeing her from this distance, through strange men's eyes.

Not beautiful exactly, her nose is too sharp and her lips are too thin, but she has something about her, cushiony curves, velvety skin, huge sea green eyes for them to drown in. At home, she's too up-close to see. I can only smell her sadness, and I need to look away. Her sadness smells of sherry.

Opposite the bar, the band's gear is set up on a low, wide stage. The drum kit dominates, a constellation of shimmering cymbals and, off to one side, an electric piano, matt black, lurking. Mum returns with soft drinks and sees me looking at the piano.

"He bought it on tick," she says. "Behind my back, paid it off when he got the redundancy money. He says he was going to tell me. But when? How much longer would he have left it?"

She looks hard at me now, as if I might actually know, as if I should be able to explain Dad to her. But it's impossible to tell her about all the nights he sat late at the piano while she was out looking after other people, the sadness in his riffs sometimes, not like the sad smell of sherry, nothing like her sherry, a blue kind of sadness that makes you want to move with the rhythm, makes you want things you can't even name.

I scan faces in the crowd waiting for the band now. "Are you sure I'm old enough to be here?"

She says, "You're with me. It's fine." She hasn't touched her orange juice.

The lights where we're sitting dim down. And I don't know where the band came from but suddenly they're on the stage, three backs turned to the audience, guitar, bass and sax, all in a huddle facing the drummer – and Dad out there alone on the far side behind the piano, peering into the crowd.

"He can't see us," Mum says. She starts to wave and I join in.

The sax and bass players turn and go to their mikes, and our waves get wider but Dad just keeps peering. Mum nudges me. "Stand up," she says. I really don't want to but she insists. "Don't be silly. He's looking for us. Stand up." She doesn't stand herself.

Dad spots me, just as the guitarist turns and her hair swings out in a golden arc. He gazes straight past her, grinning towards me and she looks over too and, for a second, her face seems to crumple. Long enough for Mum to notice? I'm not sure. When I check, she's twisting the stem of her glass, round and round and round, and she still hasn't touched a drop of the orange juice. The guitarist smiles out at the audience now, like she doesn't care that Mum and I are here. But I think she does. The band launches into "Take Five" and a ripple of recognition runs through the room. She strikes a chord and half turns to Dad and he nods to her, still smiling. I'm not sure what it means. Maybe something to do with the music.

He looks back to our table and Mum seems to relax, raises her glass at last, sips at the orange juice. And I think maybe there's a chance for him, a chance for us all. Maybe we'll survive.

36

1969

The park was deserted, grass sodden and everything dripping – silver trickles on the chute, slick black seats on swings, and the river roaring by the bottom edge, churning round rocks, spitting out spume. Me and Olive raced to the roundabout and started pushing, got it going as fast as we could before we flung ourselves on. We lay back breathless, heads together, bodies angled away from each other and our feet dangling over the rim. Drizzle spattered on our faces and the air sang in our ears as we gazed up at the dizzy sky.

When Peter showed up, he wanted on and we kept whizzing by. Now we saw him, now we didn't – his face – the chute – sky – trees – river – his face again, pale and stubborn. He made a grab for the edge of the roundabout and Olive kicked his hand away. He tried again and I got him this time. We kicked and kicked him again and again until he backed off.

Olive yelled, "Get lost, weirdo. Go home. Go on."

I raised my head to see if he got the message and caught the smirk on his face as we flew by. He wasn't going anywhere.

Next thing we knew, he was running full pelt towards us. He hurled himself on to the roundabout and thumped down in between us. I shoved him towards Olive. And she shoved him back to me, hard. His head crashed into my shoulder and I got a whiff of his hair, a disgusting salty boy smell. I wriggled out from under him and rolled as far away from both of them as I could get. What happened next had nothing to do with me.

Olive and Peter scrambled on to their knees, locked in a tussle, swaying together. No words. I can't remember any words, no yelling or anything. Maybe there were none. Or maybe they were drowned in the roar of the river, carried off all the way to the sea and you could hear them in St Andrews, while Olive backed him closer and closer to the edge of the roundabout. They were still in a tangle right up to the second Olive yanked herself away and catapulted Peter into thin air.

And for a moment, he was nowhere. Just gone.

I didn't see him until the roundabout came round again. He'd landed on his back, one leg stuck straight out, the other buckled under him. We were going too fast to get a good look at him but we weren't all that worried at first. At least there was no blood. Not like the time he braked his bike so hard he went flying headlong over the handlebars. There had been a bright red pool then. It didn't look as bad as that. We kept on whirling past him, and it was a while before we started to think it was kind of weird he still hadn't moved, and a while longer before the roundabout slowed down enough for us to jump off.

His eyes were shut, and the drizzle had darkened his strawberry blond hair to orangey brown. I stood in a puddle by his feet staring down at him while Olive circled round us yelling. "Stop acting it. Get up. Right now. Get up."

At first, I thought the same as her. He was playing dead, just like he played dumb. He was good at that kind of thing. But he had hit the ground with such a crack he should've been screaming. I didn't understand how he could keep all that noise in.

"Get up, moron." Olive prodded him in the side with the toe of her shoe. He didn't move or make a sound.

She said to me, "Where's the blood? He's putting it on."

There was no blood. If there had been blood we would've tried to help him. Olive started circling again. Behind us, the roundabout was still slowing down, screeching with every long-drawn-out rotation. She prodded his other side. Still no reaction.

I looked at Olive. "I don't think he's breathing."

She said, "Don't be daft. You can't tell from there."

I didn't argue back. I didn't want to be right and I didn't

167

want to look at him closer in case I was. Olive didn't want to look either. She started wheeling wider and wider, round the roundabout and the chute.

"What'll we do?" Her voice seesawed up and down and up. "Don't just stand there. What'll we do?"

I had no idea. I looked around the park, hoping an answer would appear out of the drizzle. Somebody out walking their dog maybe. Somebody safe and solid and grown-up who would take over. But no – this bit of rain seemed to be keeping the whole town indoors.

Olive said, "You're useless." Like she was any better. We could've got down on our knees beside him. We could've tried to lift him. But we were scared to touch him and find out he was gone for sure. We didn't want to believe it. He couldn't just stop being there. If there had been blood we would've done something quick. We wouldn't have hung about swithering. But there was no blood.

And now Olive was backing away, whining like she was the one hurt. "It wasn't our fault. He made us do it." She squeezed her eyes shut so she couldn't see him.

But somebody had to look. Somebody had to make him go on being there. I stared down at his ashen face, willing him to open his eyes.

Got you – he'd smirk. *Got you, suckers.*

And the relief would fizz and rush up through our bodies and burst out of our mouths – *you moron weirdo wee creep.* We'd really want to kill him then. For scaring us. But not so he was dead, just so he was sorry. We'd wipe the smirk right off his face. And he would deserve it.

"He made us," Olive said again. Her voice seemed to be fading and when I looked up she was still backing away, her face blurred in the soft rain. She might have been crying. It was hard to tell and anyway I didn't care. I wasn't going to share the blame, no way.

I said, "I didn't touch him." This was true. She knew it was. I was nowhere near him.

Olive didn't answer. She took another step backwards, down the grass slope towards the corner of the park and the way out. Her face was just a smear now and I couldn't tell what she was thinking.

"I didn't touch him. Don't you try and make out I did."

She stepped back again and her not speaking made me mad. I plunged down the slope towards her and she turned and ran. Of course, I knew I wouldn't catch her. I never could unless she let me. Her legs were longer, looser, faster. I skidded to a stop and yelled, "Are you going to get help?"

"I don't know." She kept going towards the park gate.

"What d'you mean? We can't just leave him."

"You stay then." I could hear her feet slapping on the sodden grass.

I turned to check on Peter, hoping hard, but he hadn't moved and the big, empty park made his body look tiny. I didn't want to stay with him and I didn't want to leave him lying there alone. Water trickled down my cheeks but it was just the drizzle. I wasn't crying yet. Olive had stopped at the park gate, and I watched her look both ways twice like she couldn't make up her mind which way to go next. Then she swung round and yelled back, "I'll say we found him, okay? We told him we'd catch up with him and when we got here he was on the ground."

She poked her head towards me. "Okay?"

The word swam through my head. *Okay?* It made my belly churn. She was talking like he was definitely dead. How could that be okay? I wanted her to tell me, but she didn't wait.

And Peter was there, but not there now. And there was nobody to see me. What did I do next? I still don't know. Nothing has ever come back.

37

1973

My first morning at the salon and I don't have an overall. Lizzie looks me up and down with cool grey eyes. "What size d'you take... ten... twelve?"

I say, "I'm not sure. It depends."

Her eyebrows shoot up and disappear beneath a cloudy, platinum fringe so pale it makes June look brassy. I bet they both know their weight and measurements down to the last inch and ounce and probably each other's as well.

June says, "Olive left an old overall that might do."

And Lizzie looks me up and down again. "It'll have to." I think she's already regretting agreeing to give me a try. She thought Olive was too intense, but Olive's not half as strange as me. At least Olive wanted to be here.

June steers me through a beaded curtain into a cluttered back room that smells of peroxide and coffee. The overall is bubblegum pink, plain except for a big white daisy printed on the patch pocket. I'm a totally different build from Olive and I don't expect it to fit, don't want it to fit, don't want to slip easily into Olive's clothes and Olive's place. And I don't want to believe it when the overall's okay, snug but not tight.

June says, "Hmm, a bit longer on you but it'll do. You may as well keep it. She's not likely to be back for it." She doesn't sound the least bit sorry Olive's gone.

I catch my reflection in the mirror above the sink. It looks all right from the neck down but my face looks wrong. Or maybe the face is fine and it's my body that doesn't go with it. The pink makes me think of skin. Not mine. I look away quickly and spend the rest of the day avoiding mirrors, which isn't easy in a hairdressing salon.

When a client arrives, I'm supposed to say – *Can I take*

your coat, madam? But I already know half of them and the "madam" keeps sticking in my throat. I have to force it out. The ones who know me say "thank you, Grace" back, and every time I hear my name it sounds like a mistake, like it doesn't belong to me, like I'm in the wrong skin. Then a woman I don't know with a headful of rollers calls me Olive when I offer her a magazine, as if Olive was the name for all Saturday girls. I flinch but I don't put her right.

Halfway through the morning, June takes me aside and says, "Try to smile when you talk to them. Lizzie's got her eye on you." She nods towards a client sitting under a hood dryer and gives me a little push.

I twist my lips into something like a smile and trudge over. "Can I get you tea or coffee, madam?"

The client looks blank. She can't hear through the noise of the dryer, and I have to try again, speak up this time, and force another smile. Knowing Lizzie's watching doesn't help.

At lunchtime, June and Lizzie and the other stylists crowd into the back room with their sandwiches. And eyebrows go up again when I take off the pink overall and put on my jacket to go out.

June says, "Olive always stayed and made everyone a cuppa."

Of course, she did. I should've guessed. Olive would do anything to make them like her. I glance towards the kettle. I'm not sure if it's okay to go or not now.

"We'll manage," Lizzie says. "You don't need to look so worried. You go and get some fresh air." I think she's glad I'm going and she wouldn't be too sorry if I never came back again.

Maybe I won't.

*

How long can I make this hour last? Walking fast takes me further from the salon, from Lizzie and June and from the pink overall, but it doesn't stretch the minutes, and it doesn't help me shake off the feeling I'm in the wrong place. Olive's place. I need time to get back into my own skin.

I hurry through the alley past Bella's cottage. Her curtains are open today. This is the first time I've thought of her by name and not just as Olive's grandma. She seems more real now I've been inside and seen a bit of how she lives. And she seems lonelier too. She'll never know why Peter and Olive are gone, or what it had to do with her, and I'll never tell her. She only knows how the story began: *Once upon a time, there was a girl named Gina who lived in a house of clocks, a house that ticked like a bomb...* I don't know what happened next, how it exploded. I can't even guess. I only know how the story ended.

I stop on the railway bridge and lean over the parapet. The signal is up and the signalman is on his feet, waiting for the express to shoot through. I can't hear it coming yet. How long can I make this hour last? If I think about nothing that's not here and now, I can stretch out a second to feel like a minute, delay the train a bit longer. But then I remember I have to get back to *Lizzie's* and the dread creeps in and time speeds up again.

DERRY OK is still there on the wall and I wonder if Olive has figured it out yet. Is she troubled by Northern Ireland these days? I don't know what Olive thinks any more but she's probably too busy surviving to worry about stuff like Ireland right now. It would be nice to believe our lives were simpler back when all we wanted to know was *who* Derry was, which one of the gang that hung around outside the snooker hall. Things were never that simple though.

At first when I heard she was gone, I thought I could start to forget. I didn't think she'd still be here in my head. But wherever I go it feels like she's there already, waiting for me to catch up. Waiting for me to understand – she'll never be completely gone until I go too. As long as I stay here in this town, the roundabout will keep spinning and Peter will fly off again and again.

The signalman looks up at me now, and I think about waving but I'm too old for that. Behind his box, the river sloshes and chugs. The InterCity roars closer and closer and the noise starts to swell until I can't tell the sounds of the river and train apart any more, both racing through, not stopping for anyone. The bridge starts to shudder as carriage after carriage thunders beneath me, and I hear Olive bawling at the top of her voice. Bawling right in my ear. *STOP. HELP.*

I turn to look but she's not there. And my mouth is wide open.

38

1969

They found me crouched next to Peter, staring into space – Mum and Gina Broadfoot and Mr Wilkie, the Provident Insurance man, who'd brought them in his car. An ambulance was on its way. But Olive hadn't come back with them. They'd made her stay with Mr Wilkie's wife, and that was no use to me. I needed Olive there with me, needed to know what she was thinking and what she'd told them and what I should say. I couldn't think straight without her.

Gina Broadfoot knelt down in the wet grass and cradled Peter's head in her lap. Mum pulled me away. I didn't want to look at her but I let her hug me anyway. She needed the comfort more than me. Because I was thinking nothing at all now. Nothing. Zero. Blank.

After a bit, she stood back and wiped the drizzle from my cheeks. "Olive said you found him?"

And I gave her the smallest nod. Any smaller and it would've been invisible to the naked eye. The smallest nod, a silent lie, but it was the biggest lie I ever told.

I thought there would be more questions later, and I was on my guard for days. But all Mum ever said was *how are you feeling? Are you okay?* It bothered her I hadn't cried. She seemed to think she knew how I should feel. Which was more than I did. The idea of "no Peter" was too enormous and I wasn't even close to crying yet. I hadn't seen Olive since the park, and I kept going to the window to stare across the square at the Broadfoots' house.

The first morning after Peter stopped being there, Olive's mum came out to scrub the front doorstep and polish their brass letter box. And later, Olive's dad pedalled off on his bicycle, head down, staring blindly at the ground. Neighbours trooped to their door with casserole dishes, and flowers, and cards. Olive's grandma showed up lugging her tartan shopping bag and left again quickly.

The second morning he stopped being there, Mum came and stood at the window with me. She said, "Wait till the funeral's by before you go over."

Of course, she was assuming I must be missing Olive. Maybe I was. I wasn't sure. I turned and looked at her. "You don't need to tell me."

She stroked my hair and said, "Good girl," which only showed how much she knew. I was glad she had to work nights. I didn't want her fussing over me. While she slept I mooched around the house, started one book then another and gave up after a few pages. I didn't care what happened next.

The third morning, I stood at the window for a while but there was still no sign of Olive and it was beginning to feel like she'd died along with Peter. I put on the telly and sat and listened to the music that went with the test card till the lunchtime news came on. The build-up to Apollo 11 had begun and a man from NASA was telling the newsman how this would be the first time human beings tried to land on another heavenly body. I knew he said *heavenly body* because the moon wasn't a planet, but I got the feeling he also said it to make the moon sound more important, like stars and moons and planets were equal, and I was suspicious of everything he said after that. In any case, Apollo 11 was not as exciting as Apollo 10 so far. School was out for the summer and there wasn't the buzz of other kids talking about it, no playground chanting down from ten to *Houston we have lift-off.*

They decided I was too young to see Peter buried and, on the fourth day, I was sent to spend the day with my godmother, Marie, while Mum and Dad and every other adult in the square attended the funeral. Marie gave me fish fingers and beans for lunch and told me it was okay to feel sad. She didn't say if it was okay to feel nothing. And I couldn't tell her how we wouldn't let him on the roundabout and how we kicked him and kicked him. I should've felt something about that. Dad had whisky on his breath when he came to take me home.

I used to practise the piano only when they made me and never at the weekends or in the school holidays, but now I didn't know what to do with myself and I started going to the piano of my own accord. I practised "Für Elise" and "Golliwog's Cakewalk", but it was Chopin's "Prelude in E Minor" I kept coming back to. There was one chord close to the end where my left hand wasn't big enough to make the stretch and I had to drop the bottom note. The piece was mournful, lonely, and I played it with the soft pedal down. Mistakes didn't sound so bad that way. I played it over and over until the notes came automatically and sorrow flowed through my fingertips and the names of Peter's favourite dinosaurs repeated in my head – Diplodocus, Pterodactyl, Triceratops, Tyrannosaurus Rex. It didn't make me cry though and I began to worry this might mean I didn't have any proper feelings. Maybe I didn't then. Maybe I still don't. Maybe there's no such thing.

The week after the funeral, one boring grey afternoon, Mum came downstairs and found me sprawled on the couch watching the test card again. She perched on the arm by my feet and said, "You're looking pale. Why don't you go over for Olive and see if she wants to go out?"

I said if she wanted, she'd come for me and went on watching the test card.

But Mum wouldn't let it go. "D'you know how selfish you sound?" she said. "Olive's lost her brother. She could do with a friend."

She got up and turned off the telly and I watched the blank screen instead. I told her I'd go over tomorrow. I didn't mean it though. I didn't see how me and Olive could go on being friends. Peter was dead and things could never be normal again. But Mum said, "Right then," and picked up the phone to speak to Olive's mum.

They didn't give us a choice. Next day, they sent us out

together with enough money to buy iced drinks in the Riverbank Café. We went to keep them happy, but it was obvious Olive didn't want to go any more than me. We didn't look at each other, didn't know what to say. We walked in silence down Springfield Road and across the railway bridge. Didn't bother to stop and wave to the signalman. Didn't go in the alley, didn't even turn to look as we went by.

We sat at a green Formica table by the café window and ordered lime iced drinks, sipped them slowly through our straws, stopping now and then to stir the ice cream in the soda and keep the mixture foaming. And still we didn't know what to say, where to start, didn't want to say his name.

In the end, I blurted out, "It was an accident. We could still tell them."

And Olive stared at me like I was crazy. "No we can't. It's too late. We can't change our story now. And anyway – why should they believe us?"

"Because it's true. You didn't do it on purpose, did you?"

She frowned, and the coffee machine behind us gurgled and hissed. "I can't remember. It happened too fast."

"But I can tell them. I can swear." I still wanted to believe it could be that simple.

"So why did we lie then?" Olive said.

"What d'you mean?"

"That's what they'll say. Why did we lie in the first place?"

I couldn't think of an answer.

"See?" Olive said.

She glugged down the dregs of her drink and left me to think about it, and the smell of roasted coffee beans wafted through the café, and "Prelude in E Minor" played in my head along with all the names of Peter's dinosaurs: Brontosaurus, Stegosaurus, Pterodactyl, and the rest, I don't know how many million years dead. Time had stopped for Peter as well now. But not for us, Olive was right. It was too late to change our story.

39

1973

Pisgah Wood wraps round me, and I breathe deeper and deeper the further in I go, sucking in the jumble of smells, the sweet and bitter greens, the musk of earth and bark. I've been holding my breath for days, holding it since the moment I heard Olive was gone. It's taken me all Sunday morning to find a way around the fence. The developers do what they like. Call it progress. And now – to get back to the wood you have to leave the town behind, hike all the way out by the dual carriageway and up through Hillside Farm.

The wood closes in. I've never gone this deep on my own before. Some folk say they're scared of the dark, as if the dark is always the same, as if seeing is all that matters, as if eyes keep you safer than noses or ears. And some folk, like Olive, won't admit that they're scared. But I always knew she was scareder than me. She needed me here in the wood beside her as much as she needed a place to hide.

And it's weird but it feels like she's here still, peering at me through the rhododendron leaves. The forest floor is knotted with oak and sycamore roots, criss-crossed with animal tracks and human paths. Every fork is a choice and I choose the narrowest path every time, let it pull me towards the heart of the wood, to the place where we used to vanish from the world together.

And now I can hear her hissing my name, trailing behind me hissing at danger, while the path grows thinner and thinner and the undergrowth thickens and tangles around us. And we're more and more lost – but that's okay. We want to be lost. Faraway from the square. Home's another life, not here, not now. The wood swallows us up, gobbles us alive and whole, and we disappear into the deep, green darkness, Olive and me, not caring if we find our way back.

Acknowledgements

The family of Helen Lamb wish to acknowledge the warm support and advice of Tracey Emerson in making this novel happen. Special thanks to Magi Gibson for her help and support to Helen throughout her writing career and in bringing *Three Kinds of Kissing* to publication. We would also like to thank everybody at Vagabond Voices, especially our editor Dana Keller.